Princess Collection

Disney PRESS
New York

TABLE OF CONTENTS

SUSTAINABLE FORESTRY INITIATIVE

Certified Chain of Custody
40% Certified Forests,
60% Certified Fiber Sourcing

www.sfiprogram.org
PWC-SFICOC-260
FOR TEXT PAGES ONLY

Disney's THE LITTLE MERMAID

Ariel's True Love

From deep underwater, a mermaid named Ariel noticed a ship sailing by above. Her father, King Triton, had warned her many times not to go to the ocean's surface. He thought humans were dangerous. But Ariel was fascinated by them: she even had a secret grotto where she kept a collection of human-made treasures, such as candlesticks and pitchers.

Sebastian, a crab who was the king's adviser, noticed the mermaid swimming to the surface. He called to her, but she ignored him. She wanted to know what was happening on the ship.

At the surface, she saw a man being presented with a statue. The other sailors called him Prince Eric.

Ariel sighed. The prince was incredibly handsome. And the statue looked just like him.

Suddenly, the clouds in front of the moon thickened. A strong wind blew across the ocean and lightning crackled in the sky.

"Hurricane a-comin'!" a sailor shouted.

Waves washed over the deck, and the ship was tossed on the sea. Lightning struck the main mast and sent it crashing to the deck in flames. Soon the whole ship was on fire. Then it exploded and Prince Eric was thrown overboard!

Ariel swam toward the wreck. She had to find the prince and save him! She spotted him floating on a plank of wood. Just then, he slipped off the board and sank beneath the waves. Ariel dived after him and used all her strength to pull him to the surface.

Before long, the sky cleared and Ariel dragged the prince onto the beach. She watched over him, concerned. "He's so beautiful," she whispered. Then she began to sing to him. Eric's eyes opened, and he caught sight of Ariel. But a second later, she was gone. She had returned to the ocean so he wouldn't find out that she was a mermaid.

Later, the prince made his way back to the palace. "A girl rescued me," he told his friend Grimsby. "She was singing. She had the most beautiful voice."

Meanwhile, beneath the waves, Ariel was thinking about Eric, too. She daydreamed and planned ways to see him again. The little mermaid was in love.

Flounder, a blue-and-yellow fish who was Ariel's best friend, led her to the grotto to show her a surprise—it was the statue of Eric!

"Oh, Flounder," Ariel cried. "You're the best!"

Ariel only had a few moments to admire the statue before her father stormed in. He had found out that Ariel had been to the surface, and he was furious!

"Contact between the human world and the merworld is strictly forbidden," he scolded her. King Triton lifted his trident and took aim at the human objects.

"Daddy, no!" Ariel cried.

A golden ray shot out from the trident and destroyed a globe. Another blast shattered a candelabrum, then a painting and some books. Finally, Triton turned his trident on the statue, which exploded into pieces.

Ariel burst into tears. Her father didn't seem to understand how important these things were to her. "Just go away!" she said.

Ariel was hurt that her father had destroyed her treasures. She knew he would never allow her to see Eric. So she decided to go see Ursula, the sea witch.

Ursula made a bargain with the mermaid. She would give Ariel legs for three days. During that time, Ariel had to get Eric to fall in love with her. If he kissed her, she would remain human, but if not, she would turn back into a mermaid— and belong to Ursula for the rest of her life.

"You can't get something for nothing," the sea witch told her. "What I want from you is your voice!"

Ursula took Ariel's voice and put it in her shell necklace. The mermaid would have to get Eric to kiss her without even speaking to him!

Now human, Ariel swam to the beach. Her friend Scuttle the

seagull found a ship's sail and some rope and made her a dress. Soon, Eric discovered her.

"You seem very familiar to me," he said. "Have we met?" For a moment, Eric thought she had rescued him from the shipwreck, but then he realized she was unable to speak. "Then you couldn't be who I thought," he said, disappointed.

But he took Ariel back to his castle anyway. She tried to adjust to life on land, but everything was so strange! She combed her hair with a fork and accidentally blew soot all over Grimsby with a pipe. Eric couldn't help but laugh.

Grimsby was glad to see the prince enjoying himself. "You know, Eric, perhaps our young guest might enjoy seeing some of the sights of the kingdom," he suggested.

"It's not a bad idea." The prince turned to Ariel. "Well, what do you say? Would you like to join me on a tour of my kingdom tomorrow?"

She nodded happily. It was like a dream come true.

The next morning, the two of them set off in the royal carriage. Ariel was thrilled. The world around her was so exciting and new! She and Eric stopped for a puppet show in town. Ariel got a new hat, two loaves of bread, boots, and some flowers. A few hours later, they climbed back into the carriage. After Eric had been driving a while, Ariel took the reins. She snapped them sharply, and the horse took off!

Ariel loved being human, and Eric was enchanted by her.

That evening, from a rowboat in a quiet lagoon, Ariel and Eric watched the sun set.

"I feel bad not knowing your name," Eric said. "Maybe I could guess." He started listing names. "Is it Mildred? Diana? Rachel?" Ariel shook her head. Then Sebastian, who was keeping a close eye on the king's daughter, went to the side of the rowboat and whispered her name into Eric's ear.

"Ariel?" the prince asked.

She nodded and took his hand. Eric leaned in. Ariel closed her eyes, and . . .

Splash!

Eric and Ariel toppled into the water. Ursula had sent her pet eels to overturn the boat. The sea witch would do whatever she could to keep the two from kissing!

"Whoa! Hang on. I've got you." Eric pulled Ariel back into the boat. But the romantic moment had passed.

That night, Eric heard the voice of the girl who'd rescued him. He went to find her and soon he had—she was named Vanessa. But the girl was really Ursula in disguise. She was using Ariel's voice to trick the prince into falling in love with her.

By the next morning, word spread around the kingdom. Eric was getting married—to Vanessa!

Ariel watched, heartbroken, as the wedding ship set sail. Not only would she never kiss Eric, but tonight he would marry another girl.

Then her friends brought terrible news. They had discovered that Vanessa was really Ursula!

Ariel knew she had to stop the wedding. She jumped into the water, but without her tail she didn't know how to swim. Flounder pulled her along as she floated on some barrels. "Don't worry, Ariel," he said. "We're going to make it!"

Just as Ariel reached the ship, Scuttle pulled at the shell necklace holding her voice. It fell from Vanessa's neck and broke. Ariel's voice returned to her. "Eric?" she asked.

"Ariel?" Eric said. "It was you all the time!"

He moved toward her to give her a kiss . . . but it was too late! The sun set and Ariel became a mermaid again. Ursula pulled her into the water.

"I lost her once. I'm not going to lose her again!" Eric cried. He battled the powerful sea witch and destroyed her.

Afterward, the prince lay on the shore, exhausted. Ariel watched him from afar. King Triton surfaced and looked at his daughter. He realized how much she loved Prince Eric. Happily, he granted Ariel her greatest wish—he gave her legs, so she could be human.

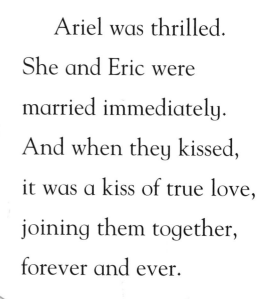

Ariel was thrilled. She and Eric were married immediately. And when they kissed, it was a kiss of true love, joining them together, forever and ever.

Walt Disney's
Snow White
and the Seven Dwarfs

Friends to Count On

Once upon a time, there lived a lovely princess named Snow White. Her wicked stepmother, the Queen, dreaded that someday Snow White would be more beautiful than she was.

Every day, the Queen asked her magic mirror, "Who is the fairest one of all?" And every day the mirror replied, "You are."

But one day, the mirror gave a different answer. "Snow White," it said.

The Queen was enraged. She ordered the royal huntsman to take Snow White into the woods and kill her.

That way, the Queen would be the most beautiful woman in the kingdom again. But the Huntsman couldn't bring himself to harm Snow White. When they got to the forest, he told the princess how much the Queen hated her. "Run away," he told her. "Hide."

Snow White turned and ran away as quickly as she could.

But the woods were scary. Branches seemed to reach for her, and roots tripped her. She felt as if eyes were staring at her from the darkness. Snow White screamed. Then she fell and buried her head in fear.

23

In the morning, Snow White lifted her head. She saw eyes watching her, but this time they were the friendly eyes of bunnies, deer, chipmunks, birds, and raccoons. Snow White was glad she wasn't alone anymore. "Please don't run away," she said. "I won't hurt you."

Snow White knew she could never return to the castle. What would she do? Where would she go? Maybe the animals can help me, she thought.

"I need a place to sleep at night," she said. The animals looked at each other. The birds took her cape in their beaks and guided her forward. Soon they came to a clearing in the woods. Beneath the trees stood a charming little cottage.

"Just like a dollhouse!" Snow White cried. She peeked in the window. No one was home. The animals nodded at her, seeming to say it was all right for her to go inside.

Snow White pushed the door open. Inside the cottage, dishes were piled high in the sink and clothes were tossed about. The floor hadn't been swept in ages. Snow White counted the tiny chairs at the table and decided seven children must live in the cottage. "Seven untidy children," she said with a shake of her head.

Snow White grabbed a broom. "We'll clean the house and surprise them," she said to the animals. "Then maybe they'll let me stay."

She started to sweep, singing all the while. The raccoons washed clothes, the deer dusted, and the chipmunks tidied. In no time, the room was spotless.

After the cleaning was done, Snow White became curious about the rest of the cottage. "Let's see what's up the stairs," she said. She lit a candle and climbed up the steps. At the top was a door. Snow White opened it and went into a room with seven little beds. Each bed had a name carved on it.

"Doc, Happy, Sneezy, Dopey," Snow White said with a laugh. "What funny names for children!" She read on. "Grumpy, Bashful, and Sleepy."

By then, Snow White was feeling awfully sleepy herself. She lay down across three of the small beds. The birds covered her with a blanket, and minutes later the princess was fast asleep.

Before long, the owners of the cottage returned. They were not children at all—they were Dwarfs.

When they opened the door, they couldn't believe their eyes! "The whole house is clean!" Doc exclaimed. Nervously, the Dwarfs tiptoed upstairs. They thought an intruder was in their room!

They went in, and Doc slowly pulled away the blanket that had been covering Snow White.

"Why, it's a girl!" he cried.

"An angel," whispered Bashful.

But Grumpy thought differently. "All females are poison!" he insisted.

As Snow White began to wake up, the nervous Dwarfs hid. They peeked at her over the footboards.

The princess yawned and sat up. Startled, she caught sight of the Dwarfs' faces. "Oh, you're little men!" she cried. "Now don't tell me who you are. Let me guess." One by one, she matched the names on the beds to the Dwarfs. She got all of them right on the first try.

Snow White told the Dwarfs how she had run through the woods and that the Queen wanted to kill her.

"Send her away!" Grumpy warned the other Dwarfs. He was worried that the Queen might use an evil magic spell on them.

"She won't find me here," the princess promised. "I'll wash and keep house and cook. . . ."

The Dwarfs imagined the apple dumplings and gooseberry pies that Snow White could make. "She stays!" they agreed. Then they followed her downstairs.

That night, after a delicious dinner, the Dwarfs and Snow White yodeled and sang. Dopey played the drums, Sleepy played the horn, and Grumpy played the pipe organ. Snow White clapped along to the music. Then she danced with her new friends. The Dwarfs had never had so much fun or laughed so hard!

When they stopped singing and dancing, Sleepy turned to Snow White. "Tell us a story," he said.

Snow White told them about a princess who had fallen in love with a prince she'd met at a wishing well. "Was it you?" they asked, and she nodded. Her dearest wish was to see him again someday.

Sighing dreamily, the Dwarfs let Snow White sleep in their cozy beds for the night. Bashful slept in a drawer, and Happy climbed into a cupboard. Doc chose the sink, while Grumpy hopped in a large pot. But they didn't mind—even Grumpy was glad that Snow White had stayed.

In the morning, the Dwarfs got ready to go to work in the mines. They were worried about leaving Snow White alone, especially after what the Queen had tried to do to her.

"I'll be all right," Snow White said. Then she kissed each of the Dwarfs good-bye.

"I'm warnin' ya . . . don't let nobody or nothin' in the house!" Grumpy ordered.

"Oh, Grumpy, you do care!" Snow White exclaimed and gave him a big kiss. He stomped away, pretending to be mad, but he had a goofy smile on his face.

That afternoon, forgetting Grumpy's warning, Snow White allowed a poor old woman into the house.

The woman gave her an apple, perfectly red and shiny. "Go on, have a bite," she urged. But the apple was not an ordinary apple, and the old woman was not an ordinary woman. She was the evil Queen in disguise, and the fruit had been poisoned!

Snow White's animal friends tried to warn her not to trust the woman, but she didn't understand. She reached out, raised the apple to her lips, and took a bite.

"Oh, I feel strange," she cried, and fell to the floor.

When the Dwarfs returned to the house, they found their friend and thought she was dead. They had no way of knowing that the spell the Queen had used was for a sleeping death, or that Love's First Kiss could wake Snow White up.

The Dwarfs could not bear to lose the princess. They built her a beautiful coffin of gold and glass, and set it in the woods where all her animal friends could visit her.

One day, a prince came by—the same prince that Snow White had met by the Wishing Well! He gazed at the girl in the glass coffin and knew her as the princess he loved. The Prince lifted the glass lid, bent down, and kissed her.

Slowly, she awakened. The Prince lifted her in his arms. Around them, the Dwarfs and animals danced and hugged and jumped for joy. Their friend was alive again—and her true love had found her!

"Good-bye," Snow White said and kissed each of the Dwarfs. She was leaving to marry the Prince, but she knew she would visit her good friends again soon.

An Enchanted Place

Once upon a time, there lived a beautiful young girl named Belle. She loved to read and could often be seen wandering through her village with a book.

Belle lived with her father, Maurice, who was an inventor. One day, he went to a fair. On the way home, a bad storm broke out and he took shelter inside a dark castle. But the master of the castle was an angry beast, and once he discovered Maurice, he would not let him leave!

Belle searched for her father when he didn't return home. She soon came to the castle and went inside. "Hello? Is anyone here?" she called as she walked through the hallways.

A wooden mantel clock and a fancy candelabrum were sitting on one of the tables. Belle didn't notice them, but they noticed her. "It's a girl!" cried Lumiere the candelabrum, once Belle had

passed. He jumped to the floor. "She's the one! The girl we have been waiting for! She's come to break the spell!"

Many years earlier, Lumiere and Cogsworth the clock had been human, along with lots of the other objects in the castle. But their master, the prince, and his castle had been put under a spell. The servants had been changed into enchanted objects, such as the clock and the candelabrum, while the prince had been turned into an awful beast. The spell could only be broken if, by his twenty-first year, the Beast fell in love with a girl who loved him back.

41

Lumiere and Cogsworth followed Belle. Before long, she came to the dungeon where her father was locked up.

"Papa!" she exclaimed. She knelt down to touch his hand.

"You must go!" Maurice cried. But already it was too late—the Beast had entered the room.

Belle was not afraid, though. "I've come for my father. Please let him out," she said sternly.

"He's my prisoner," the Beast growled.

"Take me instead," Belle offered.

"You would take his place?" the Beast asked, astonished.

Belle agreed, and the Beast dragged Maurice from his cell and sent him away.

On his way back to the dungeon, Lumiere suggested that his master find Belle a more comfortable place to stay than the cold, dark cell.

The Beast was not hard-hearted, though his manners were rough and his temper terrible. When he saw Belle sobbing, he softened. "Follow me," he demanded and led her to a much nicer room.

"Dinner!" Lumiere whispered in the Beast's ear. "Invite her to dinner!"

"You will join me for dinner!" the Beast commanded before he slammed the door shut.

Soon, some of the servants stopped by to introduce themselves. Mrs. Potts, the teapot, and her son, Chip, a teacup, offered Belle a spot of tea. She was surprised that the servants were

enchanted objects, but she liked them at once. They couldn't convince her to go to dinner, though.

Cogsworth finally broke the bad news to the Beast. "She's not coming," he said.

The Beast went to Belle's room and pounded on the door. "I thought I told you to come down to dinner!" he growled.

"I'm not hungry," Belle replied.

"Please," Cogsworth quietly urged the Beast, "attempt to be a gentleman."

"It would give me great pleasure if you would join me for dinner," the Beast managed.

But Belle still said no. She would not eat with the creature who was holding her captive. The Beast stormed off. "If she doesn't eat with me, then she doesn't eat at all!" he roared.

Later that night, Belle sneaked out of her room and tiptoed downstairs.

When she went to the kitchen, a strange sight met her eyes. All the dishes, the pots and pans, the stove, and the silverware were alive, just like the other objects she'd met.

They had been upset when she'd refused to come to dinner because they were eager to impress her. There were never guests at the castle anymore.

"I am a little hungry," Belle admitted.

"You are?" asked Mrs. Potts, who had been the castle cook. "Wake the china! I'm not about to let the poor child go hungry."

Belle had been hoping for a bite to eat. Instead, she got a full-blown feast. Beef and cheese, pie and pudding—Belle had never had such a meal! Her new friends treated her like a princess.

After dinner, Belle wanted to explore. "It's my first time in an enchanted castle," she told the servants.

Cogsworth and Lumiere led her around, showing her paintings, tapestries, and armor.

"What's up there?" Belle asked when they came to a very long staircase.

It was the west wing and everyone was forbidden to go there. Cogsworth and Lumiere tried to lead Belle in another direction, but she slipped by them and climbed the steps. Behind the door at the top was a wreck of a room. Furniture was torn apart. A painting of a handsome prince was ripped down the middle.

The only thing intact was a single rose under glass, and even its petals had started to fall off. Once the last petal fell from the rose, the spell over the castle could never be broken! But Belle didn't know about the spell.

Suddenly, the Beast's shadow fell over her.

"Get out!" he yelled and started to smash things.

Belle ran down the stairs and past Lumiere and Cogsworth. "Promise or no promise," she cried, "I can't stay here another minute!" She dashed out the front door, grabbed her horse, and rode into the dark forest. But the forest was not safe—it was full of wolves. They chased after Belle. She tried to hold them back with a stick, but they snapped it in two.

Suddenly, the Beast appeared. He growled at the wolves and tossed them right and left. They bit his neck and clawed at his fur, but he managed to fight them off. At last, the wolves ran away.

Since the Beast had gotten hurt while protecting her, Belle didn't feel right about leaving. She took him back to the castle and nursed his wounds. "Thank you for saving my life," she said.

Day by day, the Beast and Belle got to know each other better. They ate together. They played in the snow together. One day, the Beast shared his library with her. She had never seen so many books! And one evening, they danced together!

The servants were overjoyed. They could tell the Beast was falling in love with Belle . . . and Belle with the Beast.

But Belle was very concerned about her father's health. She wanted to see him.

Because the Beast loved her, he decided to let her go, even though it meant he wouldn't be able to break the spell.

With a last glance toward the Beast, Belle left the castle and went to her father.

When the villagers heard that the Beast had captured Belle, they attacked the castle, even though she'd told them how nice he'd been.

Lumiere and Cogsworth came up with a plan to defend the castle. When the villagers stormed inside, some of the enchanted furniture fell on them. Teacups poured scalding tea on their heads, cabinet doors flew open and knocked people down, and knives and forks soared through the air. The villagers ran out of the gates, screaming.

But during the fighting, the Beast had been badly hurt. Belle returned to the castle to find him wounded and dying.

"Beast!" she cried, kneeling beside him.

"Belle," he said, gasping. "You came back!" He was weak, though, and soon his eyes closed.

"Please don't leave me!" Belle sobbed. Then, just in time, she added three magic words: "I love you."

Tiny comets showered down on the Beast. As Belle watched, the Beast's claws became hands and his fur changed to human skin. He became the prince he once had been and would be again, now that Belle had broken the spell.

"Belle, it's me," he said.

She looked deep into his eyes. "It is you!" she cried happily.

Cogsworth, Lumiere, Mrs. Potts, Chip, and all the other servants returned to their human forms, too.

Belle leaned in and kissed her prince.

"Are they gonna live happily ever after, Mama?" Chip asked.

"Of course, dear," Mrs. Potts said with a happy sigh. "Of course."

Walt Disney's
Cinderella

The Mice Save the Day

One day, Gus, Jaq, and the other mice who lived in Lady Tremaine's château gathered around their friend Cinderella as she pulled her mother's old dress out of a trunk.

"Isn't it lovely?" Cinderella said. "Well, maybe it is a little old-fashioned," she added, "but I can fix that!"

Earlier that day, the mice had watched as an invitation to a royal ball arrived. Since Cinderella's father died, her stepmother, Lady Tremaine, forced her to do all the housework. But her stepmother had promised that Cinderella could go to the ball if she finished her chores and found something presentable to wear. Her mother's old dress needed a few alterations, which wouldn't be difficult—if Cinderella could find the time to do them.

"Cinderellllaa!" her stepmother and stepsisters called. They were getting ready for the ball and wouldn't give Cinderella a moment's peace. Plus, she still had to do all of her chores.

"I guess my dress will just have to wait." She sighed sadly.

After she left the attic, Jaq said, "Know what? Cinderelly not go to the ball."

The other mice looked at him, startled. Cinderella's bird friends, who were perched on the attic windowsill, twittered anxiously.

"Work, work, work!" he explained with disgust. "She'll never get her dress done."

Cinderella's animal friends decided to surprise her by fixing the dress. After all, she had been caring for them for years. Just that day, she had rescued poor Gus from a mousetrap. Then she had given him a new shirt and fed him. Every day she made sure her mouse and bird friends got enough to eat.

The mice and birds worked together to make Cinderella's dress the most beautiful at the ball. First, they measured the gown's skirt. Jaq and Gus used scissors to cut a long swatch of pink fabric. Flying through the air, the birds draped the fabric across the back of the dress. More birds hoisted the mice into the air so they could sew the fabric into place.

Then the mice hefted sewing needles over their shoulders and stitched on pretty ruffles. The birds draped on shiny ribbons. As a finishing touch, Gus and Jaq found a sash and a string of beads that the stepsisters had thrown away.

The birds and mice completed the dress just as the carriages arrived to take Lady Tremaine and her two daughters to the ball.

Sure she wouldn't be able to attend, Cinderella sadly climbed the stairs to her attic room. But when she opened the door, her animal friends called out, "Surprise!"

"Oh, thank you so much!" Cinderella exclaimed. The birds and mice were overjoyed to see their friend so happy. She was always working so hard.

When Cinderella ran downstairs in her new dress, her stepsisters and stepmother were very surprised. They hadn't thought Cinderella would find anything to wear.

"We did make a bargain, didn't we, Cinderella?" her stepmother said.

Suddenly suspicious, Jaq and Gus watched from a mouse hole in the wall.

"Those beads give it just the right touch, don't you think, Drizella?" Cinderella's stepmother asked.

"Why, you little thief!" cried Drizella. She lunged and ripped the beads off Cinderella's neck.

"Look, that's my sash!" Anastasia piped up.

The girls tore Cinderella's lovely dress to shreds and then flounced out the door to their carriage. Cinderella, her hopes dashed, ran to the garden, crying.

DISNEY PRINCESS COLLECTION

Cinderella's animal friends gathered around her as she wept on a stone bench. They wished they could comfort her.

Suddenly, Cinderella heard an unfamiliar voice say, "There, there. Dry your tears."

It was Cinderella's fairy godmother! Waving her magic wand, the Fairy Godmother turned a pumpkin into a magnificent coach.

Cinderella stared in amazement as the Fairy Godmother continued to work her magic. "Bibbidi-Bobbidi-Boo!" she cried. Soon, four of the mice, including Gus and Jaq, had turned into white horses. Bruno the dog became the footman, and the stable horse became the coachman.

Then the Fairy Godmother looked at Cinderella's torn dress. "Good heavens, child!" she exclaimed. "You can't go to the ball in that!" She waved her wand once more. Suddenly, Cinderella was wearing beautiful glass slippers and a blue ball gown that shimmered like diamonds. Even her hair was arranged elegantly. She gazed at her reflection in the fountain with disbelief.

"It's more than I ever hoped for!" she declared, her eyes sparkling.

The Fairy Godmother helped Cinderella climb into the coach. "You must understand, my dear, on the stroke of twelve the spell will be broken."

When she arrived at the palace, Cinderella felt as though she were in a dream world. Everyone wondered who this mysterious girl was.

The handsome young prince bowed before her, and Cinderella felt her heart pounding. Later, he swept her into his arms, and they danced together in the castle garden.

Gazing into her eyes, the Prince leaned down to kiss her just as the clock struck twelve. When she heard the bell toll, Cinderella remembered the Fairy Godmother's warning. She raced down the grand staircase, accidentally leaving one of her dainty glass slippers behind.

The next day, Cinderella went about her chores. She daydreamed and hummed a waltz as she worked. Cinderella's mouse friends tried to warn her to be careful, but she was too busy thinking of the Prince.

Lady Tremaine overheard Cinderella and recognized the song from the ball. She realized that Cinderella was the girl from the ball who'd danced with the Prince all evening. Her stepmother locked her in her attic room.

"No! Please let me out!" cried Cinderella.

"We've got to get that key," Jaq told Gus. The two mice raced downstairs and quietly took the key out of the stepmother's pocket. Then they pushed and pulled it up the long staircase. With a last burst of energy, Cinderella's exhausted little friends were finally able to slip the key under her locked door.

"Oh, thank you!" she cried.

Cinderella hurried down the steps. The Grand Duke had arrived while she was locked in the attic. He was searching for the Prince's mysterious love by trying the glass slipper on every maiden in the kingdom, including Cinderella's stepsisters.

"Wait, please wait!" she called to the Grand Duke.

At the sound of Cinderella's voice, everyone looked up. The mice hugged each other hopefully. But Cinderella's stepmother was upset that her stepchild had escaped, and she tripped the Grand Duke with her walking stick. The slipper Cinderella had left behind at the ball shattered!

Luckily, Cinderella still had the other slipper. She pulled it out of her pocket, then tried it on.

70

The slipper's perfect fit proved that
Cinderella was the beautiful young
woman who had won the Prince's
heart. The Prince asked for
Cinderella's hand in
marriage, and the very
next day they had
their wedding at
the palace.

Gus, Jaq, and the other mice were thrilled that Cinderella had found her true love. Cinderella insisted that her loyal animal friends move to the palace with her. They gladly left Lady Tremaine's château behind and began a new life as royal mice.

A Time for Courage

Long ago, and far beyond the Great Wall of China, a young woman named Fa Mulan lived with her family.

One day, the Emperor's aide rode into town. "The Huns have invaded China!" he announced. "One man from every family must serve in the Imperial Army."

Mulan's father felt it was his duty to join the army even though he had been injured in earlier battles. That night, he began to practice some fighting moves, unaware that Mulan was watching. Suddenly, a pain from an old wound shot through his leg, and he collapsed on the floor.

Mulan knew that her father wouldn't be able to survive another battle, so she decided to disguise herself as a man and take his place. She cut her hair, put on soldier's clothing, and left in the middle of the night on her horse, Khan.

But Mulan was not alone. The spirits of her ancestors sent Mushu, a tiny dragon, along to protect her.

Mushu caught up with Mulan and soon they arrived at the army camp. Mushu whispered suggestions about how to look more like a man. "Show them your man walk," he said. "Shoulders back, chest high, feet apart, head up, and strut."

"I don't think I can do this," whispered Mulan.

"It's all attitude," Mushu told her.

Mulan took a deep breath, gathered her courage, and strode into camp.

She looked ridiculous, but she did her best. When she tried to make friends with the other soldiers, Chien-Po, Yao, and Ling, she ended up causing a fight.

The camp was in total chaos when Captain Shang arrived.

"Soldiers!" the captain shouted.

Everyone sprang to attention and pointed at Mulan. "He started it!" they said in unison.

"I don't need anyone causing trouble in my camp," Shang said to Mulan.

"Sorry," Mulan said. Then she remembered she was supposed to be a man and lowered her voice. "I, uh, mean, sorry."

"What's your name?" Shang asked.

"My name is . . . uh . . . Ping," Mulan told him. She handed him her army papers and frowned. She was not off to a good start.

Captain Shang was a skillful leader, and though Mulan felt clumsy and inadequate, she worked as hard as she could. She didn't want anyone to find out she was a girl.

Shang led the recruits through a series of grueling training exercises to help them prepare for battle. One of the lessons involved retrieving an arrow from the top of a pole with a heavy bronze disk tied to each wrist.

"One represents discipline, the other strength," Shang said of the disks. "You need both to reach the arrow."

No one was able to do it. Finally, after several attempts, Mulan had an idea. She pulled the weights onto her wrists, looped them together, and used them to hoist herself to the top. She had done it!

All the soldiers admired Mulan's determination. And even her new friends, Chien-Po, Ling, and Yao, still didn't know that she wasn't a man.

After much training, Shang led the soldiers to the Tung-Shao Pass to meet the rest of the army. When they arrived, they discovered that the army had been defeated—and none of the soldiers had survived. Shang was especially upset when he realized that his father, the General, had been killed.

"I'm sorry," Mulan said, trying to comfort him.

Shang composed himself and turned to his soldiers. "The Huns are moving quickly. We're the only hope for the Emperor now. Move out!" he ordered.

Before long, the Huns discovered Shang and his troops. Hundreds of them raced over the mountaintop, firing arrows at Shang's small band of soldiers. Mulan seized a cannon and ran right toward the Huns. When she had almost reached their leader, Shan-Yu, Mulan aimed the cannon above his head. The rocket hit the mountain behind him and caused a huge avalanche. Snow tumbled down quickly, burying the enemy.

Mulan had been wounded, but she was still able to jump on her horse and pull Shang away from the snow just before he was buried.

As Chien-Po and the others helped them to safety, Shang looked at Mulan with admiration. "Ping, you are the craziest man I've ever met. For that, I owe you my life," he said. "From now on you have my trust."

But Mulan's wound had to be treated. It was then the soldiers learned that she was really a woman.

At that time in China, Mulan's deception was punishable by death. Shang spared her. "A life for a life," he declared. "My debt is repaid." He told her she would not be allowed to continue on with the other soldiers.

Dejected, Mulan watched the troops march away, leaving her alone with Mushu and Khan. With a heavy heart, she confided in the dragon: "I should never have left home. I just wanted to do things right, so that when I looked in the mirror I would see someone worthwhile. But I was wrong. I see nothing."

"You risked your life to help the people you love," Mushu replied. "But don't worry, things will work out."

That quiet moment was shattered when Mulan realized that Shan-Yu and a few of the Huns had survived. Racing on horseback to the Imperial City, Mulan found Shang and told him what she had seen.

"You don't belong here," he replied. "Go home."

"You have to believe me," said Mulan.

But Shang wouldn't listen. Soon, the Huns seized the Emperor and ran into the palace. Mulan turned to her friends for help. Chien-Po, Ling, and Yao tried to break down the palace door. It was no use.

"Hey, I have an idea!" Mulan called. Eager for the help of their quick-thinking friend, the soldiers let Mulan dress them as women. Then they used the sashes from their dresses to help them climb the palace columns. Shang realized that Mulan was trustworthy and joined their effort. Once inside, they attacked the unsuspecting Huns.

Together, Mulan, Shang, and the others knocked out the Hun soldiers and rescued the Emperor. Then Shang went after Shan-Yu. Furious that the Emperor had escaped, the Hun leader drew his sword.

"You took away my victory," Shan-Yu growled at Shang.

"No," said Mulan. "I did." She pulled back her hair so Shan-Yu would recognize her and Shang's life would be spared.

"The soldier from the mountains!" the Hun leader cried. He began to chase her.

Leading Shan-Yu to the top of the palace, Mulan grabbed his sword and pinned his cloak to the roof. Mushu shot toward him on a rocket. The little dragon jumped to safety just before the rocket blasted Shan-Yu into a tower of fireworks.

After the battle, the Emperor approached Mulan. "I have heard a great deal about you, Fa Mulan," he said. "You stole your father's armor, ran away from home, impersonated a soldier, deceived your commanding officer, dishonored the Chinese army, destroyed my palace, and . . . you have saved us all."

Then, he bowed to Mulan in gratitude. Stunned, everyone else did the same. "See to it that this woman is made a member of my council," the Emperor told his aide.

Mulan was honored but knew that she needed to return to her family.

"Then take this, so your family will know what you have done for me," the Emperor said, handing her a pendant with his crest on it. Then he gave her Shan-Yu's sword. "And this, so the world will know what you have done for China."

Mulan thanked the Emperor and said good-bye to her friends. It was time to go home and face her father.

At home, Mulan presented the Emperor's pendant and Shan-Yu's sword to her father. "They are gifts to honor the Fa family," she explained and bowed her head.

He put them aside and hugged Mulan. "The greatest gift and honor is having you for a daughter," he said.

Shang had followed Mulan home. He realized that his feelings for her had grown. She had been very courageous, and he admired her for it.

Mulan invited Shang to stay for dinner. He and her family celebrated, delighted everything had turned out so well.

WALT DISNEY'S

Snow White
and the Seven Dwarfs

To the Rescue!

Snow White and her prince spent nearly every day together. But one morning, the Prince told Snow White that he had to leave for a few hours.

"I'll miss you," said Snow White. She decided to spend the day in the palace gardens.

Snow White changed her dress and set about her gardening. The Prince saddled his trusty horse, Astor, and rode to the garden to bid his wife farewell.

"Take good care of my prince," Snow White said, slipping a flower into Astor's bridle.

Then she gave a flower to the Prince. "And take good care of Astor," she said. She smiled and waved as she watched them trot off.

The time flew by. Before long, Snow White looked up from the roses she was tending and saw a cloud of dust on the road. A horse was rapidly approaching.

"Oh, good!" she exclaimed. "The Prince and Astor are home early!"

She hurried toward the gate to greet them.

Imagine Snow White's surprise when she saw that Astor was alone!

"Why, where's the Prince?" she wondered out loud.

Snow White tried not to panic. But she thought the Prince had to be in some sort of trouble.

"I must go and find him!" she declared bravely.

Snow White began to walk toward the forest. When she turned around, Astor was there.

The horse stamped her hoof and nodded toward her empty saddle.

"Do you want me to get on?" Snow White asked.

Astor nodded.

Quickly, the princess pulled herself into the saddle. She barely had time to sit down before Astor was racing toward the forest!

Astor ran deeper and deeper into the woods. The princess tried not to think about what dangers might await them on the dark path ahead.

After a few moments, Snow White spotted a piece
of red cloth that was caught on a long, sharp thorn.
It was a scrap torn from the Prince's riding cloak!

And that wasn't all! As she ducked beneath a low-hanging branch, Snow White glimpsed something red in the puddle. It was the petals from the rose Snow White had given the Prince that morning! She tugged on Astor's reins, but the horse charged ahead.

Soon they had almost made it to the river. Snow White saw the Prince's feathered hat dangling from a limb above the water.

As Astor leaped across the river, Snow White reached as high as she could . . . and plucked the hat from the branch.

As Snow White clutched the Prince's hat to her chest, Astor galloped farther into the forest. Straight ahead, four eyes peered out from the shadows.

"Oh!" Snow White cried.

Astor stopped short.

"Well, *tello hair* . . . I mean, hello there!" said a familiar voice.

"Doc?" Snow White said with a sigh of relief. "I'm so very glad to see you! I think the Prince is in trouble."

"Don't worry, Princess," Doc assured her. "We can help you!"

Doc put his fingers to his lips and whistled. Within seconds, the other Dwarfs arrived. They were anxious to help Snow White.

"Let's . . . let's . . . let's—*achoo!* Let's go!" Sneezy cried.

"Oh, thank you," Snow White said. "Just follow Astor," she added. "She seems to know the way."

The Seven Dwarfs and their ponies followed Snow White and Astor through the depths of the forest and over a deep, rocky canyon.

"Ooh," said Bashful, looking down. "I hope the Prince isn't down there."

Finally, they came to a sunny clearing, and Astor slowed to a stop. Snow White spotted the Prince, lying on the ground. "Oh, no!" she cried.

She slipped out of the saddle and ran toward the Prince.

"Don't worry!" she called. "I'm coming!"

Just as Snow White reached the Prince, he sat up and stretched. "What a nice nap!" he said. "And what a lovely way to awake. I hope you're hungry!"

Snow White was bewildered. Next to the Prince lay a lavish picnic.

"I knew Astor would get you here quickly," the Prince said, beaming. "I even left some clues along the way."

Snow White smiled. The Prince had planned a lovely surprise—the afternoon had turned out wonderfully. She was so glad he was all right.

The Prince noticed that the Seven Dwarfs were already digging into the delicious food. "Well," he said with a laugh, "I'm glad I brought a little extra."

"Wait until I tell you about my trip here," Snow White said as she hugged the Prince. "You'll never believe it!"

DISNEY'S
Aladdin

The Princess Who
Didn't Want to Marry

As she sat by the fountain in the palace courtyard, Princess Jasmine giggled at her pet tiger, Rajah. The tiger had not been impressed with the latest prince to ask for Jasmine's hand in marriage, so he'd helped scare him away. They were both glad to be rid of the selfish suitor, one of many unworthy princes who'd visited recently.

Jasmine's father, the Sultan of Agrabah, was not amused. "Dearest, you've got to stop rejecting every suitor who comes to call," he told his daughter. "The law says you must be married to a prince by your next birthday. You've only got three more days!"

But Jasmine thought the law was unfair. "Father, I hate being forced into this," she said. "If I do marry, I want it to be for love."

Lately she'd found herself wishing she weren't a princess at all. She had never even been allowed to go outside the palace walls. She felt trapped.

That night, the princess decided to run away. She put on a disguise and began to climb over the palace wall. Rajah tugged on her dress—he didn't want her to leave.

Jasmine knew she would miss her friend, but she had to see what else was out there.

"I'm sorry, Rajah, but I can't stay here and have my life lived for me," she explained.

Rajah nodded and slid his head under Jasmine's foot to give her a boost over the wall.

The next morning, Jasmine arrived at the marketplace. She looked around excitedly, for she had never seen anything like it. People were selling everything from pots and necklaces to fish and figs. As she walked, she came upon a little boy who looked like he hadn't eaten in a while.

"Oh, you must be hungry," Jasmine said. The boy looked up at her eagerly. She took an apple from a nearby stand and handed it to the poor child.

"You'd better be able to pay for that," the apple seller said.

"Pay?" Jasmine said with surprise. She'd never needed to pay for anything at the palace.

"No one steals from my cart!" the vendor bellowed and grabbed her angrily. Jasmine was frightened and didn't know what to do.

113

Luckily, a handsome stranger came to her rescue.

"Oh, thank you, kind sir," the young man said to the apple seller. "I'm so glad you found her. I've been looking all over."

Jasmine looked puzzled. "What are you doing?" she whispered to the young man. She noticed he had a pet monkey with him.

"Just play along," he replied.

"You know this girl?" the seller asked him.

"Sadly, yes. She is my sister," he replied. "She's a little crazy. She thinks the monkey is the Sultan."

Jasmine knelt down. "Oh, wise Sultan," she said to the monkey, "how may I serve you?"

"Tragic, isn't it?" the young man said as Jasmine pretended to be crazy. "Now come along, sis. Time to go see the doctor."

They started to leave. It looked like they would escape until the monkey bowed good-bye . . . and a bunch of stolen apples tumbled from his vest!

"Come back here, you little thieves!" the fruit seller yelled.
The trio ran as quickly as they could and finally reached the
young man's rooftop home. They were safe . . . for now.

Jasmine looked around. The stranger's home was simple, but at least it was his own. No one told him what to do. Jasmine couldn't imagine having so much freedom.

At the same time, the young man was looking longingly at the palace in the distance. It would be wonderful to live there, he thought, to have enough money so he wouldn't have to worry about his next meal.

"Sometimes I just feel so trapped," they both said.

Surprised, they looked at each other. Jasmine suddenly felt that she had a lot in common with this handsome stranger. But just then, angry palace guards burst in. Jasmine looked around—there was no escape!

"Do you trust me?" asked the young man, holding out his hand to her.

She looked into his brown eyes and said, "Yes."

"Then, jump!" he cried.

Jasmine took his hand and they leaped off the roof. They landed safely in a pile of grain, then raced through the marketplace . . . right into another set of guards!

The head guard seized the young man. "It's the dungeon for you, boy!" he declared.

"Unhand him!" demanded Jasmine, pulling down her hood and revealing herself as the princess. The guard was shocked to see her outside the palace walls. "Do as I command," she ordered. "Release him."

"I would, Princess, except my orders come from Jafar," the guard replied. "You'll have to take it up with him."

Jasmine crossed her arms and narrowed her eyes. "Believe me, I will," she said.

Back at the palace, the princess confronted Jafar, one of her father's advisers. The evil man told her that the stranger had been sentenced to death and killed.

"I am exceedingly sorry, Princess," Jafar lied.

Jasmine glared at Jafar. "How could you?" she said and ran out. She went to see her tiger friend. "It's all my fault, Rajah," she said, sobbing. "I didn't even know his name."

The next day, on the streets of Agrabah, there was a magnificent parade. Men playing drums marched down the street, followed by women dancing with scarves. All of the townspeople stopped what they were doing to watch.

Inside the palace, the Sultan heard the music. He went to his balcony and was delighted by what he saw below. "Oh, Jafar!" he called. "You must come and see this!"

Reluctantly, Jafar joined the Sultan.

Trumpets blared and banners waved as the parade made its way to the palace. But most impressive was Prince Ali, who sat on top of an enormous elephant, throwing gold coins into the crowd. He looked attractive, regal—and extremely smug.

Princess Jasmine, who was still upset about the death of the young man from the market, watched from her balcony. She shook her head in disgust at this latest suitor. Did he think he could buy her hand in marriage?

Nevertheless, the Sultan welcomed Prince Ali into the palace. "Your Majesty, I have journeyed from afar to seek your daughter's hand," said Prince Ali after flying in on a magic carpet.

"Prince Ali Ababwa," said the Sultan, "I'm delighted to meet you."

But Jafar had his own sneaky plan: he wanted to marry the princess himself so that someday he would rule the kingdom. He whispered to the Sultan, "What makes him think he is worthy of the princess?"

Confidently, Prince Ali replied, "Just let her meet me. I'll win your daughter."

But Jasmine had been listening and was very upset. "How dare you—all of you! Standing around deciding my future," she cried. "I am not a prize to be won!" She turned and stormed off.

But Prince Ali would not give up. That evening, he appeared on Jasmine's balcony and apologized. Rajah growled protectively and was about to chase him away, but Jasmine thought the prince looked familiar. When she stepped closer, he offered to take her on a magic carpet ride.

"We could get out of the palace . . . see the world," Prince Ali offered.

Jasmine hesitated. "Is it safe?" she asked, looking at the carpet.

Prince Ali leaned forward, offering his hand. "Do you trust me?" he asked. Jasmine thought he might be the young man from the marketplace! Maybe he hadn't been killed, after all! She gave him her hand and climbed aboard the Magic Carpet.

Jasmine and Prince Ali flew over the streets and rooftops of Agrabah. They held hands, and Jasmine felt happier than she ever had.

Jasmine got the prince to admit he was the young man from the marketplace. But he didn't tell her everything because he didn't think she would like him if she knew the truth. His real name was Aladdin. After escaping from the dungeon, he'd found a magic lamp. The Genie inside had given him three wishes. Aladdin, who had fallen in love with Jasmine, had used one of them to become a prince so he could marry her.

"I sometimes dress as a commoner to escape the pressures of palace life," he lied. "But I really am a prince."

"Why didn't you just tell me?" asked Jasmine.

"Well, you know, uh, royalty going out into the city in disguise . . . it sounds a little strange, don't you think?" he said.

Jasmine looked down. "Not that strange," she said quietly.

Soon after they returned from the romantic magic carpet ride, Jafar discovered Prince Ali's secret and revealed his true identity. Then Jafar tried to seize power, but Aladdin and Jasmine fought him bravely and won. Together, they had saved the kingdom.

After the battle, Aladdin took Jasmine's hands in his. "I'm sorry I lied to you about being a prince," he said humbly.

Jasmine held his hands. She hadn't fallen in love with him because she thought he was a prince. She loved him for who he was inside. The princess had finally found someone she wanted to marry. Her father gladly changed the law so that she'd be able to.

Aladdin and Jasmine climbed aboard the Magic Carpet and kissed. Beneath them was a whole new world where they would live together, happily ever after.

Walt Disney's
Sleeping Beauty

Falling in Love

Once upon a time, in a faraway land, there lived a king and queen. They longed to have a child and, after years of waiting, their wish was granted. A daughter was born. They named her Aurora after the dawn, because she filled their life with sunshine.

To celebrate her birth, the king and queen declared a holiday. Guests traveled from near and far to visit the tiny princess, including three good fairies named Flora, Fauna, and Merryweather.

Each fairy would bless the princess with a single, magical gift. Flora blessed the child with beauty. Fauna gave the gift of song. But before Merryweather could cast her spell, a gust of wind blew through the great hall.

In a flash of lightning, a tall, dark figure appeared. It was the evil fairy Maleficent, who was furious that she hadn't been invited to the party.

"I, too, have a gift to bestow on the child," she said with a wicked grin. "Before the sun sets on her sixteenth birthday, she shall prick her finger on the spindle of a spinning wheel and die!" And with that, she disappeared in a burst of foul green smoke.

The king and queen were panic-stricken. Flora tried to calm them. "Don't despair," she said. "Merryweather still has her gift to give."

Although her magic was not strong enough to undo the curse, Merryweather did have the power to help.

And so, with a wave of her magic wand, Merryweather declared, "Not in death, but just in sleep the fateful prophecy you'll keep. From this slumber you shall wake, when True Love's Kiss the spell shall break."

Still, the fairies thought, perhaps there was an even better way to save the princess from the curse. What if they pretended to be peasant

women and raised the princess as their own in a secret, far-off place for sixteen years? If Maleficent could not find Aurora, how could she harm her?

The king and queen sadly agreed to the plan, knowing it was the only way they could protect their daughter from Maleficent. They watched with heavy hearts as the fairies changed themselves into humans and disappeared into the night with the princess.

By morning, the fairies and the princess arrived at an old cottage deep in the woods, which became their home. The fairies stopped using magic and pretended to be Aurora's aunts. They called her Briar Rose, so no one would learn of her whereabouts. That would keep her safe from Maleficent.

The years passed quickly and before they knew it, Briar Rose's sixteenth birthday arrived. To celebrate, the fairies planned a surprise—they would make the girl a beautiful dress and a delicious cake! But first they had to get her out of the cottage. So they sent her to pick berries.

Briar Rose enjoyed strolling through the woods. As she walked, she sang to the forest animals who had become her friends, all the while dreaming of a tall, handsome prince.

Little did she know that a real prince just happened to be riding through the forest that very morning.

"Hear that?" the prince said to his horse, Samson. The sound of Briar Rose's sweet voice had drifted over to him. The prince was enchanted—he had to find out where it was coming from!

Eagerly, he urged his horse into a gallop—but as Samson leaped over a log, the prince fell off. He landed in a creek with a most undignified splash.

"No carrots for you!" he scolded as he climbed out of the water. He laid his hat, cape, and boots out to dry. At the same time, he couldn't help but wonder about the voice he'd heard. It was almost too beautiful to be real.

"Maybe it was some mysterious being," he said, "a wood sprite, or a—"

But his thoughts were interrupted by the shocking sight of his wet clothes beginning to fly and hop away. Briar Rose's animal friends were stealing them!

"Why, it's my dream prince!" Briar Rose laughingly declared when the rabbits and birds appeared before her, dressed in the stolen clothes. "You know, I'm really not supposed to speak to strangers, but we have met before." And while the real prince looked on, hidden behind a nearby tree, Briar Rose began to sing and dance with her dressed-up forest friends.

As Briar Rose turned away, the real prince quickly stepped in. When he began to sing with her, she spun around.

"Oh!" she gasped. Her three aunts were always warning her to stay away from strangers . . . and yet there was something so familiar about this young man (whom she never dreamed was an actual prince). She couldn't help but feel that they had met before.

Long into the afternoon, Briar Rose and the prince sang and danced together, and before either one could help it, they had fallen in love.

When Briar Rose finally returned to the surprise party that awaited her at the cottage, it was her aunts who were most surprised.

"This is the happiest day of my life," Briar Rose said with a sigh. Then she told them about the young man she'd just met, and how she'd invited him to the cottage that very evening.

"This is terrible," moaned Flora. "You must never see that young man again." She explained to Briar Rose that she was already betrothed—and had been since birth—to a young prince named Phillip.

"But how could I marry a prince?" Briar Rose asked. "I'd have to be . . ."

". . . a princess," Merryweather finished.

The fairies then told Briar Rose about her real parents and her real name. Flora, Fauna, and Merryweather changed themselves back into fairies, wrapped the princess in a cloak, and set off for the palace immediately.

They arrived at the castle just as the sun began to set. The poor princess was so sad about not being able to see the young man from the forest again that the fairies left her for a moment so she could collect herself. As soon as they were gone, a wisp of green smoke appeared and lured Aurora up a tower to a hidden room.

Slowly, the smoke took the form of a spindle, and Maleficent's voice filled the air. "Touch the spindle!" she ordered. Aurora pricked her finger on the spinning wheel and fell into a deep sleep. The only thing that could save her was True Love's Kiss.

Unfortunately, Maleficent had locked the prince in her dungeon. The good fairies found him and discovered that he was Prince Phillip, the same prince who was betrothed to Aurora! They gave him enchanted weapons with which to fight Maleficent. Though the evil fairy changed herself into a fierce dragon, she was no match for the prince's bravery—or the magic sword and shield. He soon defeated her.

Prince Phillip raced to the palace and knelt beside the sleeping beauty. Ever so gently, he kissed her on the lips. He sighed with relief as she opened her eyes and smiled at him.

Soon, a grand, joyous wedding was announced. True love had conquered all!

Disney's THE LITTLE MERMAID

Where's Flounder?

"Ready or not, here I come!" Ariel called out. The red-haired mermaid turned, opened her eyes, and looked around for any sign of her friend Flounder. They were playing hide-and-seek, and Ariel was "it."

She looked behind some seaweed, checked around some pink coral, and peeked inside a clamshell. Ariel didn't find the yellow-and-blue-striped fish, but she did find another little fish.

"Did you see which way Flounder went?" she asked the blue-and-orange fish.

The fish pointed a fin toward the palace where Ariel lived. "Oh, thank you!" the little mermaid cried as she swam that way.

Once inside, she zoomed around looking for her friend.

"Ariel!" King Triton exclaimed as his daughter swam into the room. He held his arms out to hug her, but she raced past him. "So nice to see you. But I gather you've come to visit someone else?"

"Oh, hello, Daddy," Ariel replied. "Flounder and I are playing hide-and-seek." Then she noticed something move by the table. It must be Flounder! she thought. She swam over and moved a piece of seaweed. A sea horse smiled at her.

Ariel frowned. "Have you seen Flounder anywhere?" she asked her father.

King Triton smiled slyly. "I *may* have seen him," he said. "And I *may not* have seen him," he added jokingly.

Hmmm . . . thought Ariel. This is no help at all. Where could Flounder be? Then she had an idea—maybe he was up on the surface.

"See you later!" she called to her father as she quickly swam away.

Up at the surface, Ariel found Scuttle the seagull, but no Flounder.

"Hi, Scuttle!" said Ariel.

"Hi, Ariel!" Scuttle replied. "I haven't seen Flounder."

Ariel eyed Scuttle suspiciously. "Hey . . . how did you know I was looking for him?"

Scuttle held up his wings in surrender. "Okay, okay!" he cried. "You forced it out of me! He came by looking for a hiding place. But then he headed off toward your secret grotto."

"Thanks, Scuttle!" Ariel said and dived back underwater.

Ariel swam to her secret grotto. She loved human things like beads and lampshades. Sometimes Flounder helped her on treasure hunts. Whenever they found something new, they would take it to the grotto. Ariel searched all around the cave, but she didn't find Flounder.

Soon, she gave up and headed back to the palace. On her way back, she saw a pretty piece of coral and stopped to admire it. Behind the coral was the red crab who was one of her father's most trusted advisers.

"Sebastian!" Ariel exclaimed, slightly startled.

"Ariel!" Sebastian replied. "What in the world is going on? First, Flounder comes tearing through here, and then you come along and scare me half out of my shell! All I want is some peace and quiet!"

"Sorry, Sebastian," Ariel replied. "But did you see where Flounder went?"

"He swam in that direction," said Sebastian, pointing a claw. "Why?" he called out. "What's happening?" But Ariel was gone with a flick of her tail.

Hmm, thought Ariel, as she swam in the direction Sebastian had pointed to. The only good place to hide out this way would be . . . the sunken ship! But Flounder was afraid of the creepy old ship. He avoided it whenever he could. Why in the world would he hide there?

Then it hit Ariel: because it was the very last place she would look for him!

The mermaid searched the whole ship—opening doors, peering around corners, and peeking under loose floorboards. She found some starfish, but there was no sign of Flounder, until . . .

. . . Ariel heard a soft "ahem."

"Flounder," Ariel said with a giggle as she swam toward the noise. It seemed to have come from inside a cupboard. She pulled the door open and saw her friend. She'd found him at last! "Gotcha!" she cried. "You picked a great hiding place."

Flounder smiled at Ariel.

"But now that I found you," Ariel said, "it's your turn to be 'it'!"

Flounder turned and began to count as Ariel swam off to find a hiding place of her own. . . .

Disney's
POCAHONTAS

LISTEN TO YOUR HEART

One day, an adventurous young woman named Pocahontas journeyed deep into the forest to visit Grandmother Willow, an ancient spirit.

Pocahontas told the wise tree that she was troubled by a dream she kept having about a spinning arrow. "It spins faster and faster, until suddenly it stops."

"It seems to me this spinning arrow is pointing down your path," Grandmother Willow replied.

"But what is my path?" wondered Pocahontas. "How am I ever going to find it?"

Grandmother Willow smiled warmly. "All around you are spirits, child," she said. "They live in the earth, the water, the sky. If you listen, they will guide you."

Later, Pocahontas thought about what Grandmother Willow had said. In the distance, she saw something. It was a ship filled with settlers from England.

The next day, Pocahontas spotted a man exploring the forest. His name was John Smith and, like the other men on the ship, he had sailed to this new land in search of gold.

Pocahontas was curious about this man— she had never seen anyone like him before. So she followed him through the woods. Suddenly, he seemed to disappear behind a waterfall. Pocahontas crept out from her hiding place cautiously. Smith jumped through the falls and came face-to-face with the young woman. The two stared at each other for a while. Smith had never seen anyone so beautiful. He moved closer, but Pocahontas was frightened and ran away.

"Wait! Please!" Smith called as he ran after her. "It's all right. I'm not going to hurt you."

Pocahontas hesitated. Leaves swirled around the pair as Smith moved closer and offered her his hand. "Who are you?" he asked.

"I'm Pocahontas," she replied as she took his outstretched hand. When they touched, neither one wanted to let go. In her heart, Pocahontas knew that there was something special about this strange man.

Together, they laughed at Meeko, Pocahontas's mischievous raccoon friend, who rummaged through Smith's bag looking for food.

Pocahontas began to sing as she led John Smith through the forest. She showed him how all the parts of nature—animals, plants, the wind, the people—were alive and connected to each other. They watched the gentleness of a mother bear with her cubs. They listened to the wolves cry and saw eagles fly to the top of a sycamore tree.

John Smith began to realize that his people had much to learn. With Pocahontas as his teacher, he could hear the voices of the mountains and even see colors in the wind. He held her hands and gazed into her brown eyes.

Suddenly, drums echoed throughout the forest. Pocahontas looked alarmed.

"What is it?" asked John Smith.

"The drums . . . they mean trouble," she said. "I shouldn't be here."

"Please don't leave," he urged.

"I'm sorry. I have to go," she said and ran off.

Back at the village, Pocahontas's father, Chief Powhatan, warned her to stay close by. "Now is not the time to be running off," he said. He didn't want Pocahontas to get hurt if fighting broke out between the settlers and the Indians.

"Yes, Father," said Pocahontas.

Later, when Pocahontas and her friend Nakoma were gathering corn, John Smith appeared.

"Please don't say anything," Pocahontas whispered to her friend before leaving with Smith.

Nakoma was too shocked to respond. She kept quiet but felt uncomfortable as she watched the two figures disappear into the evening shadows. She had been warned that the settlers were dangerous and was worried about her friend.

Pocahontas led Smith to Grandmother Willow. "Hello, John Smith," the tree said.

John Smith's mouth dropped open. "Pocahontas, that tree is talking to me," he said.

"Then you should talk back," Pocahontas said, smiling.

Grandmother Willow looked kindly into Smith's blue eyes. "He has a good soul," she told Pocahontas, "and he's handsome, too."

John Smith laughed. "Oh, I like her," he said.

Pocahontas was glad the tree spirit approved. After John Smith had left, Grandmother Willow told her that she might have found her path.

Later, when Pocahontas met up with Nakoma, her friend pleaded with her not to see John Smith anymore.

"If you go out there, you'll be turning your back on your own people," Nakoma warned.

"I'm trying to help my people," said Pocahontas.

"Pocahontas, please," Nakoma begged. "You're my best friend. I don't want you to get hurt."

"I won't. I know what I'm doing," replied Pocahontas as she went back into the woods.

But Nakoma wasn't convinced. Concerned about her friend's safety, she sent an Indian warrior named Kocoum to look for Pocahontas in the woods.

Kocoum soon found Pocahontas and Smith. The warrior attacked Smith. All of a sudden, another settler showed up and killed Kocoum!

Furious, other warriors arrived and took John Smith prisoner. He was sentenced to die the next morning.

That night, Pocahontas visited John Smith. "I'm so sorry," she told him, crying. "It would have been better if we'd never met. None of this would have happened."

"Pocahontas, look at me," he said tenderly. "I'd rather die tomorrow than live a hundred years without knowing you."

163

Pocahontas left and went to see Grandmother Willow. "I feel so lost," she told the tree spirit.

Meeko's ears perked up. The raccoon brought Pocahontas a compass he had taken from John Smith's bag. The arrow on it began to spin.

"It's the arrow from your dream," the tree spirit observed.

"It was pointing to him," Pocahontas said.

"You know your path, child," said Grandmother Willow. "Now follow it."

Pocahontas ran back to the village. Just as John Smith was about to be killed, she stepped in front of him.

"If you kill him, you'll have to kill me, too," she declared to her father. "This is where the path of hatred has brought us. This is the path I choose. What will yours be?"

Everyone stared in stunned silence. Finally, inspired by Pocahontas, the chief ordered the release of John Smith.

But the fighting was not over quite yet. When one of the settlers shot at Pocahontas's father, Smith threw himself in front of the chief and took the bullet himself. In order to have his wound treated, he had to return to London.

Smith looked at Pocahontas. "Come with me?" he asked.

She turned to her father for guidance.

"You must choose your own path," the chief said.

As Pocahontas watched the settlers and Indians begin to share food, she knew what her path must be.

"I'm needed here," she decided.

"Then I'll stay with you," Smith replied.

Pocahontas shook her head. "No. You have to go back," she told him.

"But I can't leave you," he said sadly.

"You never will," she told him. "No matter what happens, I'll always be with you." Then she kissed him good-bye—forever.

As the ship set sail, Pocahontas stood atop a cliff. She was proud that she had listened to her heart, even if it was the hardest thing she had ever done.

Disney's Beauty and the Beast
Sweet Surprises

When the bells on the door of the Jolie Bakery jingled, Claire, the baker's daughter, looked up from behind the counter. Her face lit up when she saw who it was.

"*Bonjour*, Belle!" Claire sang out. "I was hoping you might stop by today."

Belle gave her young friend a warm smile and set down the stack of books she was carrying. "Mmm," Belle said, inhaling deeply, "and just in time for some fresh chocolate croissants, I see!"

Claire chose a pastry for each of them and brought the plates over to a little table in the corner.

"Are those new?" she asked Belle hopefully, pointing to the books. Belle often stopped by and read to Claire after a visit to the library. Claire loved listening to tales of faraway places as she iced cakes or rolled out dough.

"Actually, those are the ones we already read," Belle told her. "I'm about to return them." Then, seeing the disappointment on Claire's face, she added, "Shall I make up a story instead?"

"Yes, please!" Claire replied. "But let's eat our croissants first."

"Mmm," Belle said when they had finished, "I just love chocolate."

Then, while Claire iced a cake, Belle concocted a fairy tale about a flying purple dragon, an ancient wizard, and a clever princess who freed the entire kingdom from an evil spell.

"I wish I could make up stories like that," Claire said with a sigh.

"Have you ever tried?" Belle asked.

They went to the back room so Claire could prepare the day's bread deliveries. "Sometimes I can think of a beginning to a story, but not an end," the little girl admitted. "And sometimes I can come up with an end, but not a beginning. At other times, all I can think of is the middle! I don't have a very good imagination."

Claire's father, Henri, overheard them. "*Ma chérie*," he said, "do not worry so much about imagination. You have a lot of it—you just need to figure out how best to use it."

"*Oui*, Papa," Claire said thoughtfully.

Before long, the bread was ready. Belle offered to help Claire deliver it.

As they wheeled the bread cart around town, Belle and Claire passed the dressmaker's shop. In the window was a very fancy dress. "It looks like a wedding cake," Claire remarked. Belle looked at the dress. Claire was right. The skirt was made of tiers of satin, and the pink ribbons looked like icing.

"Madame designs all of the gowns herself," Claire said. "She's so talented!"

"Indeed she is," Belle agreed. "Each dress is different from the next. She must be filled with ideas!"

As they passed the florist's shop, Claire admired a bouquet.

"Aren't these pretty?" Claire asked. "Madame Fleuret is so good at putting the right flowers and colors together."

Belle nodded, but she noticed that Claire seemed troubled. As they left the shop, Belle asked her friend what was wrong.

"Everyone in our village is good at something—except for me," Claire blurted out.

"What do you mean?" asked Belle.

Claire took a deep breath. "You can make up wonderful stories. The dressmaker can design beautiful dresses. And Madame Fleuret can take a bunch of ordinary flowers and turn them into a work of art."

"You're an excellent baker," Belle pointed out.

"But I want to make something beautiful and creative," Claire said.

From that moment on, Claire was determined to find a hobby that let her create something unique.

The next time Belle walked into the bakery, Claire rushed out from behind the counter and handed her friend a big box with a bow on top.

"For you!" Claire said proudly. "I designed it myself."

"Why, thank you!" Belle replied, surprised. She untied the ribbon, lifted the lid off the box, and pulled out a dress.

But what a dress! It was sewn from patches of mismatched fabric. One sleeve was attached down near the waist. And the buttons were all out of place.

Belle didn't know what to say. Luckily, Claire said it for her.

"Goodness, it's ugly—isn't it?" the little girl said, starting to laugh.

"Well, it is unusual," Belle said with a giggle.

She offered to try it on, but Claire wouldn't hear of it.

"Bad news," Claire announced to Belle a few days later. "I tried writing poetry, but I'm terrible."

"Are you sure?" asked Belle as she sat down on the steps of the bakery.

"Just listen," Claire said, then she read aloud:

"Sometimes when I roll out the dough,

The rolling pin drops on my toes.

While in the oven the tart bakes,

Alas, my foot still throbs and aches!"

"You're good at writing a funny poem," Belle pointed out.

"That's just the problem," Claire replied sadly. "I wasn't trying to be funny." She paused. "I'll just try something else."

The following afternoon, Claire arrived at the cottage where Belle lived with her father, Maurice. The girl was wearing an artist's smock and carrying a canvas under her arm.

"I want you to be completely honest," she told Belle as she unrolled a portrait she had just painted.

"It's . . . um . . . very interesting," Belle said. "Is it Madame Fleuret's dog, Gigi?" she guessed.

"It's you," Claire confessed.

"Well, of course it is!" agreed Belle. "I just didn't recognize myself with that different—and very pretty—new hairstyle you gave me."

Claire sighed. "Belle, thank you for being so nice, but the truth is, I'm not good at painting either."

179

"Don't worry, Claire," Belle reassured her. "It's just like your dad said—you just haven't found the best way to use your imagination. You'll figure it out soon."

"I don't know, Belle," Claire replied, frowning. "It seems like I've tried everything."

Just then, Maurice called to his daughter. Belle and Claire went to his workshop and found him tinkering with an odd contraption. It was his latest invention. It looked like a bicycle with an engine, dials, an exhaust pipe—and a miniature trumpet for a horn!

Beep! Beep! Maurice tested the horn. "Look!" he cried. "It's a vroomicycle, to help people get places more quickly."

"That's great, Papa!" Belle cried. "I've got to run, though. It's time to walk Claire back into town."

"Why does your dad invent things?" Claire asked Belle as they walked toward the bakery.

"He can't help it," Belle answered. "When he looks at an ordinary object, he sees how it might become new and different."

The next morning, Belle arrived at the bakery very early. It was Maurice's birthday, and she was going to help Claire bake a cake. As the little girl cracked eggs, sifted flour, and whipped up a custard filling, Belle practiced with the pastry bag.

Squirt! The custard landed all over Claire's father.

"Mmmmm," Henri said, tasting it. "*Magnifique!*"

When the cake was done, Belle thanked Claire for her hard work. "My father will love it," she said.

Suddenly, Claire clapped her hands together. "I know how to make this a cake Monsieur Maurice will never forget!" she cried.

Claire quickly made more cake, frosting, and filling. Then she added it all to Maurice's cake. When she was done, the cake looked a lot like Maurice's invention!

"Claire!" exclaimed Belle. "Don't you see? Baking is where your creativity shines through!"

Claire beamed proudly. She *did* have a good imagination— and now she knew how best to use it!

A couple of days later, Belle went into town and saw a crowd in front of the bakery window. When she joined them, she saw what they were so interested in—loaves of bread shaped like swans and cakes that resembled fancy hats.

The next day, Belle walked by the bakery again. Another crowd was gathered by the window. This time, they were looking at a huge cake in the shape of a castle. The drawbridge was made of peppermint sticks, and the flowered vines that climbed up the castle walls were really pieces of candy.

Belle entered the bakery. "Claire, your baking is the talk of the town!" she exclaimed.

Claire smiled. "Remember when you said your father doesn't just see what's in front of him—but what it might become? I've been looking at bread and cake every day without realizing I could turn them into something extraspecial."

Belle turned to Henri. "What do you think of Claire's creations?" she asked.

"I think they are the product of a wonderful imagination!" the baker replied. Then he winked and added, "She gets that from me, you know!"

Sleeping Beauty

Briar Rose to the Rescue

One morning, Briar Rose awoke with a yawn. A bird was singing at her window. She looked at the pretty flowers that had started to grow near the cottage. Somehow, it seemed different outside.

After she had dressed, she went to the kitchen to greet her three aunts—Flora, Fauna, and Merryweather.

"Good morning, dear!" Flora cried.

"It's the first day of spring!" Fauna exclaimed.

"Oh, I thought it looked awfully pleasant outside," Briar Rose remarked as she sat down at the table.

Merryweather placed a biscuit with extra honey in front of the young woman. "You slept late again," she said, frowning. "The day is half over."

Briar Rose smiled. Her aunt sounded grumpy sometimes, but she knew Merryweather had a heart of gold.

"I suppose we have to do our spring cleaning today," Merryweather added.

"Yes, dear," replied Fauna. "That's what we always do on the first day of spring."

"I'm afraid we're going to need a new broom," Flora said suddenly. "The one we have is quite ragged and dirty from all our winter cleaning."

"Why don't I make a new one?" Briar Rose offered. "I'll go out and find some straw and a nice, straight, sturdy stick. You'll have a new broom in no time!"

"Why, that's very sweet of you!" Flora cried.

"Dress warmly, my dear," Fauna said. "It's still cold out, you know."

"Don't stay out long," Merryweather added. "You'll leave all the work for us!"

Briar Rose tried hard not to giggle. She knew that her aunt Merryweather wasn't worried about the work. She just wanted to make sure Briar Rose was safe.

Briar Rose wrapped her cloak around her, picked up her basket, and went outside.

In the shed, she gathered straw for the new broom. As she put it into her basket, two little chipmunks appeared and began to chatter.

"Well, come on, then," she said, inviting them along. The chipmunks jumped into the basket.

Then some cheery bluebirds chirped at her from the rafters. "You can come, too," Briar Rose offered. They were joined by other birds and animals, and soon everyone was parading happily through the woods. Briar Rose began to hum. She loved to walk with her animal friends.

As they got closer to the pond, Briar Rose noticed a flutter of activity. She started to worry. What could be causing such a commotion?

The bluebirds flew ahead to see what was going on. The chipmunks jumped out of the basket and joined a group of animals that were gathered around the pond. Briar Rose ran as fast as she could. When she caught up, she saw that a deer had fallen through the ice and couldn't get out!

Briar Rose knew this deer well—it was a doe that was going to give birth very soon. She had to help the poor animal, but she wasn't quite sure how.

Thinking quickly, Briar Rose hurried over to a fallen tree and broke off a long, sturdy branch. She stretched it toward the deer.

The deer tried to reach the branch, but she had lost a lot of her strength and seemed panicked. Briar Rose wondered what she could do to help.

Suddenly, she had an idea. She began to sing the softest, most soothing lullaby she could think of. The doe started to calm down. Then the tired creature was able to grasp the branch in her mouth. Briar Rose tugged and pulled until the doe climbed up onto the bank of the pond at last.

Briar Rose sighed with relief. Then she realized how badly the deer was shaking!

"Oh, you poor thing!" she cried. "You're half-frozen!" She pulled a big handful of straw from her basket and rubbed it briskly over the deer's body. The doe's coat slowly began to dry, but she was still shivering.

"Come on, everyone!" Briar Rose announced. She and the other animals led the deer through the woods. When they reached her aunts' cottage, Briar Rose took the doe directly to the warm fireplace. The deer left a trail of muddy hoofprints all over the floor.

"We'll have to clean all over again," said Merryweather.

"Oh, phooey!" cried Fauna. "Who cares about all that? How can we help, Briar Rose?"

"She fell through the—" Briar Rose started to say.

"Hmph! I knew something like that would happen," Merryweather interrupted.

"We need to get her warm—" continued Briar Rose.

"And dry, and fed," Flora interrupted.

Briar Rose and her aunts worked together to make the deer comfortable. By the next morning, the animal felt much better.

Later that spring, the doe gave birth to two beautiful fawns. Flora and Fauna were delighted, although Merryweather still griped about how long it had taken to clean the muddy hoofprints up.

One morning, Briar Rose went to the shed to start her chores and noticed Merryweather giving treats to the deer. She smiled. That was just like her aunt, pretending to be annoyed, but actually acting very thoughtful. Briar Rose went about her chores, delighted that the spring had gotten off to a nice start.

A Royal Friend

"The princess is coming!" a crowd of girls exclaimed as they watched Cinderella's carriage come down the hill toward their school.

"Let me see! Let me see!" cried Emma, who had arrived at the school only a few days earlier. "I want to see the princess!"

"Don't worry, you will," replied Claire, who was the oldest. "She's coming to visit us."

Sure enough, the coach came to a stop right outside.

A royal trumpeter blew his horn loudly to announce Cinderella's arrival at the school.

"Quickly, girls, gather around," said the headmistress of the school. She scurried to the door and opened it wide. "Welcome, Your Highness!" she exclaimed. She and the girls curtsied as Cinderella entered the room.

"It's so nice to see you all again," said the princess.

Cinderella liked to stop by the school to help the girls with their reading and writing. She also brought books, clothes, toys, and food. Many of the girls were poor and had few things of their own.

Everyone was happy to see Cinderella. But no one was more excited than Emma.

Cinderella and the girls spent a wonderful afternoon together. After their lessons, they sang and danced and told stories. Then they read together, shared sweets, and played with some of the toys the princess had brought.

When it was time for Cinderella to go, she gathered the children together and made an announcement. "In one week's time, there will be a grand ball at the castle—to be held in your honor."

"For us? Yay!" the girls shouted excitedly. Emma and some of the others even clapped.

"But what will we wear?" asked a girl named Annabelle. She had on a dress that had patches on it.

Cinderella smiled. "Why, the dresses I am having made for each of you, of course! And you shall have new shoes and gloves as well! I remember how much fun it was when I got to dress up for the ball where I met the Prince. I thought all of you would like to wear fancy gowns, too."

The next day, the girls talked about nothing but the party. They couldn't wait to dress up.

"Do you think my gown will be blue to match my eyes?" asked Claire.

"I hope there will be lots of yummy cake and candy to eat!" said Annabelle.

"I wonder how I should wear my hair," Emma remarked.

That afternoon, the headmistress decided to take the girls outside for some fresh air. "It's a lovely day," she announced. "Let's have a picnic."

The girls climbed the hill and spread blankets in the meadow near the royal estate. While her classmates ran and played, Emma gazed at the castle. I can't wait to see what it looks like inside, she said to herself. It must be the most wonderful place in the whole world.

Soon, Emma noticed a group of seamstresses approaching the castle gates. Hmm, she thought, maybe when they go inside I can peek at the courtyard. She ran over by the castle and hid.

The women spoke with the guard. He opened the gates and let them in. Without thinking, Emma slipped behind the seamstresses and followed them straight through the courtyard and into the castle! Then she hid behind a curtain.

Cinderella welcomed the women, then led them up a sweeping staircase. When everyone was gone, Emma slipped out from her hiding place, ran up the stairs, and began to explore. One room had a huge bed with a pink, ruffled canopy. She climbed onto it and closed her eyes for a moment.

Cinderella's mouse friends, Jaq, Gus, and Mary, quickly came out from under the bed. They introduced themselves to Emma, who smiled, stood up, and curtsied.

Suddenly, they heard a voice declare, "This fabric is gorgeous!" It came from a room down the hall.

Emma and the mice went to the room and peeked around the doorway. Seamstresses were cutting satin, silk, and velvet inside.

"Everything is so pretty!" Emma blurted out.

"Come in! Come in!" the seamstresses called.

"Stand here, dear. Now, hold still," one of the women said as she began draping fabric around Emma. She thought Cinderella had sent her to model the dresses.

Emma just smiled. She loved the swishing sound the cloth made and the smooth feel of the gown. She also liked the way everyone fussed over her.

When Cinderella stopped by a while later, Emma was barely visible beneath all the satin and lace. "More bows, please," Emma requested. "And another layer of ruffles."

"Oh, my!" exclaimed Cinderella. "That certainly is a fancy dress! And you look beautiful in it."

She thought Emma had come to the castle with the seamstresses and that she must be tired from working all afternoon. Cinderella remembered what it was like to do chores all day. So she invited Emma to have tea with her.

Cinderella and Emma went downstairs to the dining room, where they sat at a table laid with delicate china and gleaming silver. A servant brought in tea and cakes and cookies, and soon the princess and the little girl were chatting like old friends.

"It must be wonderful to be a princess," Emma said between bites. "You get to wear fancy clothes, live in a big castle, go to parties all day, and order servants around."

Cinderella laughed. "When a princess wants something, she asks politely. And there's much more to being a princess than clothes and parties," she replied. "Why don't you help me this afternoon and see what a princess *really* does?"

For the next few hours, Emma and Cinderella put together baskets of food, clothing, books, and toys for schools and orphanages around the kingdom.

Emma's favorite part was going through Cinderella's wardrobe to look for old clothes that could be donated.

She put on a long velvet cape and twirled around in front of the mirror. "Look at me!" she cried.

"You look positively stunning!" said Cinderella, laughing.

211

Soon, it was time to deliver the baskets. Emma climbed into the royal carriage beside Cinderella. As they passed through the village, the little girl leaned out the window and waved at a passerby.

Princess Emma, she thought. I like the sound of that!

When they arrived at her school to deliver some baskets, the headmistress gave Emma a big hug.

"Where have you been?" she cried. "We've been so worried." The headmistress and the other girls had been looking for Emma all afternoon.

"But I thought she was with the seamstresses," Cinderella said, puzzled.

Emma explained how she'd snuck into the castle. "I'm sorry," she said. "I didn't mean to make anyone worry. I just wanted to see what it was like to be a princess."

"Being a princess is more than just playing dress-up," Cinderella told her. "It also means being responsible. "Why don't you come to the castle when you've finished your studies each day?" Cinderella suggested. "Then you can learn more about what it's really like to be a princess."

"I'd love to," Emma agreed. After that, every afternoon when her lessons were over, she went to the castle. The princess was always very busy making sure things ran smoothly, and bringing supplies to the poor and hungry. Emma saw that being a princess wasn't easy, and she admired Cinderella even more.

Emma's favorite task was helping Cinderella plan the party for the girls' school. "May we serve little cakes with pink icing?" Emma asked, thinking of the girls' favorite treats.

"Of course!" cried Cinderella. "You're a thoughtful friend to know what the other girls would like."

Meanwhile, Jaq, Gus, and Mary had been busy, too. They secretly sewed extra beads and ribbons onto Emma's dress. "Because she likes things fancy," said Jaq.

When the mice presented Emma with the dress, she clapped her hands together with delight. "It's fit for a princess!" she exclaimed.

Finally, the night of the ball arrived. The girls twirled across the dance floor in their magnificent new dresses.

"I still wish I could be a real princess," said Emma.

"Because you've worked so hard, I'm going to make you an honorary princess for the evening," Cinderella said with a smile.

"Oh, thank you!" the girl cried happily, thrilled that she'd get to be Princess Emma for one magical night.

Disney's Aladdin

Jasmine
and the Star
of Persia

Every night, Princess Jasmine and her husband, Aladdin, would sit on the Magic Carpet and gaze up at the twinkling sky above them. Then Aladdin would tell a story.

"What about that star?" Jasmine asked one evening. "The violet one."

"Ah, that," said Aladdin, "is the Star of Persia . . . named after the legendary jewel—the biggest, most beautiful amethyst in the world."

"Jewel?" said Jasmine, her eyes wide with curiosity.

"According to the legend," Aladdin began, "the Star of Persia belonged to a beautiful queen who was wise and fair and kind.

"But, alas," Aladdin said with a sigh, "not even great queens can live forever. When this queen died, her subjects hid the jewel in a tower, sure that there would never be one worthy of its beauty again."

Jasmine's eyes twinkled. "Tell me, is that story true?"

Aladdin shrugged. "I don't know. But there is one way to find out . . . if you really want to."

Jasmine smiled. "Of course I do!"

Early the next morning, Jasmine, Aladdin, and their monkey, Abu, set off on the Magic Carpet.

They flew east and before long, they were
soaring over a tiny kingdom.

"Look!" Jasmine called, pointing
to a tower. "I wonder if that's
where the queen's jewel is hidden."

When Jasmine and Aladdin touched down, they discovered that the tower was taller than they'd thought. Iron bars were on the windows and a thick chain was fastened around the door. It was clear that without a key (or at least a clever genie) there was little chance of getting in.

All of a sudden, the grumpy-looking guard standing next to the door spoke up. "What do you want?" he demanded.

Jasmine and Aladdin looked at each other. Then Jasmine walked up to the guard and smiled. "We've heard about the Star of Persia," she explained, "and we've come to see the jewel."

"I'm afraid that's impossible," the guard said. "If you've heard the legend, you should know that no one can see the jewel except a queen as lovely and worthy as our own."

"Ah," said Aladdin. "Well, please allow me to introduce you to the lovely Princess Jasmine. She's not a queen yet, but she will be one day."

Abu gestured proudly at Jasmine, who blushed.

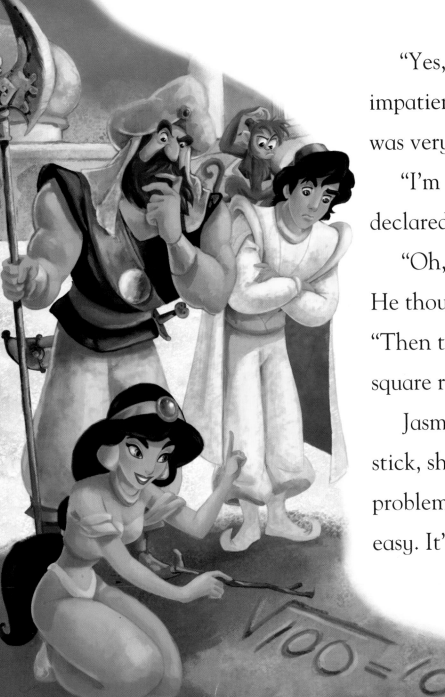

"Yes, yes," the guard said impatiently. "But our queen was very wise."

"I'm wise, too!" Jasmine declared.

"Oh, yes?" said the guard. He thought for a moment. "Then tell me—what is the square root of one hundred?"

Jasmine smiled. Using a stick, she wrote out the math problem in the sand. "That's easy. It's ten, of course!"

"That's correct," said the guard. Then his eyes narrowed once again. "But the answer is still no. After all, our queen was not only wise, she was fair, as well."

"I'm fair," Jasmine assured him.

"Fair enough to solve that argument over there?" the guard asked pointing to two men who were quarreling.

226

"Yes, I think so." Jasmine nodded and went over to the men. After a few minutes, she'd helped them make a deal. When Jasmine walked away, the two men were smiling at each other.

"You did well," admitted the guard. "But the answer is still no. For our queen was not only wise and fair . . ." He paused for a moment to sniff and wipe away a tear. "She was also very kind."

"Ah," said Jasmine, placing her hand on his shoulder. "You still miss her, don't you?"

Then she turned to Aladdin. "Let's not bother him anymore," she said. "I'll go get him a drink from that fountain over there. He must get thirsty standing in the sun all day. Once I do that, we can be on our way."

Jasmine hurried to the fountain, which she was surprised to find quite dry. To her relief, however, as soon as she held a jar under it, a stream of cool, clear water came bubbling out.

Then, her jar full, she turned to take it to the guard—only to find him and everyone else in the plaza gathered around her, staring.

"What?" she asked. "Did I do something wrong?"

"The fountain!" blurted the guard. "It hasn't given water since our dear queen was alive! Did you know that only she could make it work?"

"Why, no!" said Jasmine with surprise.

"Many a queen," the guard went on, "has been wise and fair and even kind. But no one else has ever been able to get water from this well." As the people bowed, the guard drew a key from his pocket.

The guard unlocked the chains barring the tower door. He led Jasmine up a staircase to a room high at the top. There, on a pedestal, bright enough to light the sky, sat the gleaming Star of Persia.

"Oh!" Jasmine exclaimed. "It's the most beautiful thing I've ever seen!"

"It is beautiful, isn't it?" said the guard. "And I know how happy our queen would be to know it won't be hidden any longer."

"What do you mean?" asked Jasmine.

"I mean," said the guard, "that you have proved yourself worthy, Princess Jasmine, to call it your own." And with that, he picked up the jewel and offered it to her.

She put it on at once.

233

"How can I ever thank you?" she asked.

"By enjoying it," said the guard, "just as our queen did. And promise to come visit us whenever you can."

"Oh, I will! I will!" exclaimed Jasmine. "I'll be sure to wear the Star of Persia." She waved to the guard and the townspeople from the Magic Carpet. What a wonderful day they'd had, and now Jasmine had an incredible story of her own to tell.

Belle's Special Treat

"And from that moment on, the princess had flowers every day of her life. The End,'" Belle read, and closed the book with a sigh.

"What a treat!" she said to the Beast. She gazed out the library window at the cold, snowy hills. "The winter is lovely, of course . . . but I'd give anything to have flowers every day. Wouldn't you?"

The Beast looked surprised. Flowers every day? He hadn't really given it any thought. He'd had so much else on his mind, after all. But he really wanted Belle to be happy at his castle. He wondered what he could do about it. Then he remembered something. He had a greenhouse! He just hadn't been there for years.

Later that night, after Belle had gone to sleep, the Beast decided to go to the greenhouse. He tiptoed down the hall, grabbed Lumiere the candelabrum, and headed into the snowy night.

"Are we really going where I think we're going?" Lumiere asked enthusiastically, as he lit the Beast's way.

His master only nodded. All of a sudden, the Beast was worried. What if the flowers he'd once taken such pride in (*too* much pride, many had said) had died from loneliness and neglect. They were, after all, rare and delicate species, collected from almost every corner of the world. And the Beast hadn't laid eyes on them since the day the enchantress had cast her spell on him and his castle. He just hadn't seen the point of caring for flowers anymore—especially when no one would be coming to compliment them.

Cogsworth the clock looked out the window as the Beast and Lumiere went by. What if the master needed something from the castle? he wondered. Lumiere wouldn't be able to leave him outside in the dark to go get it.

Cogsworth decided he'd better see if he could do anything to help, especially if the Beast was doing something to win Belle's heart. If it worked, maybe she would fall in love with him, and the spell over the castle would be broken. Quietly, the clock slipped outside and followed the Beast and Lumiere.

The Beast stepped through the snow and finally reached the greenhouse.

He threw the door open and looked around. Plants were overgrown and flopped over, and leaves were everywhere.

"Ooh-la-la!" Lumiere exclaimed. "The greenhouse has changed a lot."

"Yes," the Beast replied, "but the flowers are all still alive."

Fortunately, the gardener, who was now a trowel, and his assistants, who had been transformed into a pair of clippers and a watering can, had cared for the flowers as best they could.

"There's still a lot of work to be done," the Beast told Lumiere.

Just then, Cogsworth rushed in. "Allow me to help. I know Belle will love these flowers."

The Beast nodded, and they began to work.

The Beast worked in the greenhouse for days. He slipped away with Lumiere and Cogsworth whenever he thought Belle wouldn't notice.

He dug in the dirt, trimmed the plants, and pulled out weeds. Soon, flowers were blooming like never before!

The Beast decided it was time to surprise Belle. He wanted her to have a day she would never forget.

One morning, Belle woke up and saw that Mrs. Potts the teapot, her teacup son Chip, and the Wardrobe had brought her some daffodils.

"But it's still snowing outside," she said, utterly bewildered. "Where did these come from?"

Mrs. Potts just smiled. "Have a cup of tea, then, love," she said.

Belle smiled back and leaned forward to smell the beautiful flowers. What a special treat! It's a wonderful way to start the morning, she thought to herself.

That day, Belle discovered flowers all over the castle. There were tulips in the dining room, lilies in the library, and six different colors of roses in the ballroom. Each bouquet was beautifully arranged.

"It's all too mysterious and wonderful, isn't it?" she said to Chip.

And yet, something was missing. . . . Why wasn't her friend the Beast here to enjoy these precious gifts with her?

Finally, just as the sun was setting, Belle heard a knock on her bedroom door.

244

It was the Beast.

"Where have you been?" Belle exclaimed. "I missed you."

"Really?" The Beast looked surprised.

"Really," Belle assured him. "I wanted to tell you about—"

Just then, Belle noticed leaves in the Beast's thick fur and on his cape.

"Why, the flowers are from *you*!" she exclaimed.

"Oh, um . . ." the Beast answered gruffly. Then he added, "There's something I'd like to show you . . . that is, if you're willing."

"Of course," Belle said with a smile.

The Beast led Belle to the greenhouse. The colorful blooms nearly took her breath away.

"I'd almost forgotten about this place," the Beast confessed, "that is, until you reminded me. Then I realized there *was* a way to have flowers every day."

"I don't know how to thank you," Belle said, still amazed.

"Just enjoy them," the Beast told her. "I did this to make you happy."

Belle smiled, glad to have the Beast as a friend.

A Rich Friendship

The marketplace of Agrabah bustled with activity. Merchants showed off piles of ripe fruit, cheeses, dates, and freshly baked bread. Shoppers wandered among the stands, deciding what to buy.

A girl named Jenna watched them enviously. Her stomach rumbled, but she had no money to buy food. She looked at the hungry faces of Rafi and Salima, her younger brother and sister. "Wait for me back home," she told them. "I'll go find us something to eat."

Salima and Rafi headed down a dusty alleyway to the makeshift tent the children called home.

248

Jenna walked through the marketplace, keeping her eyes open for spare coins that might have been dropped. When she didn't find any, she continued along the dirt road, hoping to spot some food. Soon, she came to the grand palace where the Sultan and his family lived.

Imagine living in a place like that, Jenna said to herself. You'd need a map to find your way from one room to the other! I bet you'd get to eat whatever you wanted, too.

She daydreamed about going to a grand feast there.

As she got closer to the palace, Jenna noticed an old apple tree towering above the wall that surrounded the gardens. One of its gnarled branches was so heavy with fruit, it nearly reached the ground.

Lunch! Jenna thought, her spirits rising.

She hoisted herself onto the low-hanging branch. Quickly, she began to pick apples and toss them gently down. She climbed higher and higher until she found herself at the top of the wall. Now Jenna could see into the palace gardens.

Everywhere she looked, Jenna saw exotic flowers. "It's . . . paradise!" she exclaimed.

A tiny parrot flew down and perched on a nearby branch. "Come here, little one," cooed Jenna. "I won't hurt you." She leaned over, trying to coax the adorable green bird onto her outstretched finger.

Suddenly, Jenna lost her balance and tumbled down into the garden. To her astonishment, she landed on something soft and furry. She turned and found herself staring into the face of a huge tiger!

Jenna just smiled. She wasn't afraid of any animals—not even a tiger. "Thank you for not catching me in your mouth," she said. "Those are some big teeth you have!"

"Are you all right?" asked a friendly voice.

Jenna looked up to see a beautiful young woman with long, flowing hair standing before her.

"Hello, I'm Princess Jasmine," the woman said. "And I see you've met Rajah."

Jenna couldn't help but stare at Jasmine's lovely silk clothing and slippers, and her sparkling crown. "I'm Jenna," she said at last, climbing off Rajah's back.

Jenna tried to stand up, but she felt a sharp pain in her ankle. Jasmine saw her wince. "You're hurt!" Jasmine cried. "Please come inside."

"No, thank you. I'm used to taking care of myself," Jenna insisted, politely but firmly. But when she tried to walk, her ankle gave out. Princess Jasmine caught her by the arm.

"You're in no condition to go anywhere, Jenna," Jasmine announced. "You're coming inside with me, and that's that!" The princess took the girl to a luxurious room inside.

Before long, the royal doctor arrived. It turned out that Jenna had twisted her ankle. "She'll have to stay off it for a few days," he told Jasmine.

"But I can't!" cried Jenna. "My brother and sister are waiting for me!"

"They can stay here. My husband, Aladdin, and I have plenty of room for everyone," Jasmine assured her.

"My brother and sister are my responsibility," Jenna declared. "We do not accept charity."

Jasmine saw the pride in Jenna's eyes. "Who said anything about charity?" the princess said. "There's a lot of work to be done at the palace, and I could use your help."

Later that day, Jenna looked out the open window and saw a blur of color flying toward her. "What on earth?" she exclaimed. As it got closer, she saw her younger brother and sister riding on a magic carpet!

"Wow!" shouted Rafi as he hopped off the rug and into the palace room. "That was an amazing ride!"

"And lots faster than a camel!" Salima cried. "The Magic Carpet took us on a tour of Agrabah. It was lots of fun. I wish you could have come."

Jenna smiled. She couldn't remember the last time she'd seen her brother and sister so happy.

Jasmine escorted the children to the baths so they could get cleaned up. When Rafi and Salima were reunited with Jenna, she scarcely recognized them. Their skin was scrubbed, their hair was brushed, and they wore beautiful new clothes.

Later, Jasmine invited the children to eat dinner with her family. The princess could tell by how much Salima and Rafi ate that they were even hungrier than she thought.

Jenna, however, ate little. Jasmine is kind, Jenna thought, but when my ankle is better, we will have to leave. It's better not to get used to fine clothes and delicious food.

Then Jenna heard Aladdin say to Rafi, "Your home is in

Agrabah Alley? My monkey Abu and I used to live on a rooftop over there. Have you ever had a run-in with old Mr. Kabali? He hates it if you so much as look at one of his apples unless you have money to pay for it."

Princess Jasmine is married to someone who used to live on the streets? Jenna thought, startled. It seemed too incredible to believe. Maybe that meant there was hope for the three of them.

The next day, Jasmine asked Jenna, Salima, and Rafi to come with her to see the palace menagerie. "There's something I need your help with," she told Jenna.

"Of course," replied Jenna, anxious to repay Jasmine for her kindness.

The moment they arrived, animals began to gather around Jenna. A giraffe nuzzled her cheek, and two baby monkeys, who had come to investigate, settled on her shoulders.

"You seem to have a special way with animals," observed Jasmine. "That giraffe is usually very timid. She hardly ever walks up to anyone."

"Oh, yes," Salima piped up. "Our parents used to say that Jenna got along well with wild animals because she is just as fierce as they are!"

Rafi nodded in agreement.

Jasmine gestured to a corner of the garden. "That baby elephant was brought to us recently. He was found wandering alone. We have tried to make him feel at home here, but he seems so unhappy. I'm not sure what else to do," the princess explained.

Jenna approached the elephant, but he turned away from her. So the girl sat down on the ground nearby and waited . . . and waited. At dusk, the elephant was still in a corner by himself. That evening, Jenna stood at her balcony and watched the lonely creature, wondering how to become his friend.

For the next two days, Jenna stayed near the elephant from morning until night, sometimes sitting quietly, sometimes petting him, sometimes speaking softly. On the third day, something wonderful happened. The elephant stood up, smiled, and pointed his trunk at Jenna. Then he showered her with water!

"Well, *hello* to you, too!" Jenna exclaimed, laughing.

After a few more days in Jenna's care, the baby elephant no longer seemed scared. He played with the other animals and even let Jenna climb onto his back.

A week later, Jenna's ankle had completely healed.

"You have been very kind," the girl explained to Jasmine. "But it's time for us to go home."

"Won't you stay here?" the princess asked. "We need someone to help care for the palace animals, and you have a special gift."

Before Jenna could answer, the baby elephant used his trunk to push her straight into Jasmine's arms!

"Thank you," Jenna told the princess, smiling. "We would be honored."

Ariel and the
Aquamarine Jewel

One glorious summer morning, Ariel was enjoying a walk along the beach. She was just about to return to the palace when her toe struck something hard in the sand.

"Ouch!" she cried, still not entirely used to the feel of human feet. After all, it hadn't been that long since she'd been a mermaid.

She looked down and saw something gleaming. She moved a layer of seaweed and picked it up.

"Whatcha got there, Princess?" her friend Scuttle the seagull asked. "Looks like a piece of that sweet gnobblybloop you humans like so much." Then, he stuck out his tongue and licked it! *Blagh!*

Ariel laughed. "I think you mean 'candy,'" she told her friend. "And no, I don't think it's that. I think it's a *jewel*!" she cried.

Since the jewel had been wrapped in seaweed and was lying on the shore, perhaps it had come from the sea!

"Scuttle," she said, "please go find Sebastian and ask him to get my father."

The seagull flew off and found Sebastian the crab, who summoned the king.

A short while later, Ariel's father, King Triton, emerged from beneath the waves.

"Ariel, my dear," declared the king, "Sebastian said you called."

"Yes, Father," said Ariel. "You see, I found this lovely jewel and—"

King Triton looked astonished. "Where in the sea did you find it?" he asked.

"Actually," said Ariel, "I found it on the shore. Do you know where it came from?"

"I can *show* you," said the king sadly. "But I'll have to change you back into a mermaid to do it."

With a blast from his mighty trident, that's exactly what he did!

Gripping the water-colored jewel, Ariel dove into the sea after her father. She'd nearly forgotten how wonderful it felt to be there. By the time she and King Triton reached the gates of Atlantica, she felt very comfortable. It was as if she'd never left.

"Why, Father," Ariel cried excitedly, "this jewel is from Atlantica!"

Ariel's excitement faded, however, when her father led her to his throne room.

"Why, it looks as if a tidal wave has been through here!" she said with a gasp. "And Atlantica's treasure—it's gone!"

"Alas," King Triton said sadly, "it's true. Can you believe it? For a thousand years, this chest has kept our kingdom's treasures safe. And then one giant wave comes and washes it all away! That aquamarine is just one of dozens of gems that were lost to us, I'm afraid. And though we've been searching ever since, it's still the only one that's ever been found."

"Don't worry, Father," said Ariel. "I'll help you find the other jewels! After all, I'm a pretty good treasure hunter, if I do say so myself!" And with a swish of her tail, she was off.

First, Ariel decided to search the old sunken ship—a place she still knew like the back of her fin. She swam in and out of the galleon until she had found close to a dozen of the missing jewels!

Next, it was off to the coral reef, where it was easy to understand how jewels could be overlooked among all the deep crevasses and bright colors. But with a little help from her friend Flounder and some other dear old friends, more lost jewels were found.

In fact, by the time the tide turned, Atlantica's treasure chest was full once more.

"Ariel, on behalf of Atlantica, I thank you," said King Triton.

"I'm just glad all the jewels are back where they belong," she replied.

The king thought for a moment. "Actually," he said, "I'm not

sure that they *are* all where they belong . . . quite yet." He reached into the treasure chest and pulled out the beautiful aquamarine that Ariel had found on the beach.

Giving Ariel a kiss on the top of her head, King Triton placed the jewel around her neck.

Then it was time for Ariel to swim back to her own castle and become a human princess once again.

She said good-bye to her father at the beach.

That night, Ariel told Prince Eric about the lost jewels, the tidal wave, and how wonderful it had felt to swim home with her father and to help Atlantica.

As she gazed out at the sea, Ariel touched the aquamarine jewel hanging around her neck. She knew that her father and the rest of her family were never far away. Even so, it felt good to have a piece of Atlantica with her, always.

Walt Disney's Cinderella

The Heart of a Champion

One day, Cinderella was visiting her old friend Frou in the royal stable when her mouse friends, Jaq and Gus, told her that a messenger had arrived at the palace! Cinderella said good-bye to Frou and the other horses and hurried off to hear the news.

It seemed there was going to be a horse show. The King usually entered it, but he never did very well. Now that Cinderella was part of the family, he thought she would be the perfect person to represent them.

"Why, I'd be delighted," Cinderella said when the King suggested it.

The next thing Cinderella knew, the King was leading her back to the royal stable. The Prince and the Grand Duke went with them.

"The finest horsewoman in the kingdom must have the finest horse in the kingdom," the King said. "I have a stable full of champions, my dear. We'll choose the best of the best, and you can begin training right away. Ah, yes! I can see those blue ribbons already!"

The King ordered his groomsmen to saddle up his horses—all one hundred and twenty-two of them—and bring them out to the courtyard.

Cinderella climbed onto the back of the first horse. She knew the stallion was the King's favorite. But he was just a bit too small. The next horse, however, was too big.

Cinderella sat on one horse after another, but none of them were quite right.

Finally, Cinderella dashed back into the stable. "I'll be right back!" she called. "I know the perfect horse!"

Moments later, Cinderella returned, leading Frou!

The King stared at Cinderella and Frou in disbelief.

"Frou may be old," said Cinderella, patting the horse's shaggy mane, "but he has the heart of a champion!"

The first thing Frou did, however, was trip over a nearby water trough. Cinderella flew over his head. She landed in the trough with a *splash*! The other horses whinnied with laughter. Frou hung his head.

"Don't worry," Cinderella said to the King. "By next week, we'll be ready."

Cinderella and Frou trained for hours each day.

But Frou kept making mistakes. No matter how sweetly Cinderella urged him, he missed every jump.

And no matter how firmly she steered him, he went the wrong way every time.

"Oh, Frou," Cinderella said, patting his head, "I know you can do it!"

No one else was quite so sure—especially Frou!

Suddenly, Cinderella's fairy godmother appeared.

"I overheard your little mouse friends talking," she explained.

"They said you need a miracle. So, here I am!"

Cinderella laughed and shook her head. "Oh, that's kind of you," she said. "But we don't need a miracle, just a good night's sleep."

"My dear," her fairy godmother whispered, "*you* know Frou can win, and *I* know Frou can win, but our friend Frou doesn't believe in himself yet. I'm going to help."

With that, she raised her magic wand and waved it at Frou. Suddenly, Cinderella and Frou had new outfits! A glass horseshoe appeared on each of Frou's hooves! "With these horseshoes, you'll never miss a step," the Fairy Godmother said.

The next day at the horse show, Cinderella saw more fine horses than she ever had before. They all looked like champions—but so did Frou! He held his head up high and stamped his hooves proudly. The King could hardly believe that Frou was the same horse he'd been watching trip and stumble all week long.

Frou cleared every jump with ease. He never took an awkward step or a wrong turn. He even managed a graceful little bow at the end.

Cinderella smiled. Her fairy godmother had been right. Frou had only needed a reason to believe in himself.

In the end, there was no question about who belonged in the winner's circle—Princess Cinderella and Frou!

"You know," the King told the Grand Duke, "I had a special feeling about that horse all along. . . ."

After the horse show, Frou returned to his stall at the palace stable, with his head a little higher, his back a little straighter, and his glass shoes ready for the next time duty called.

WALT DISNEY'S
Snow White
and the Seven Dwarfs
A Royal Visit

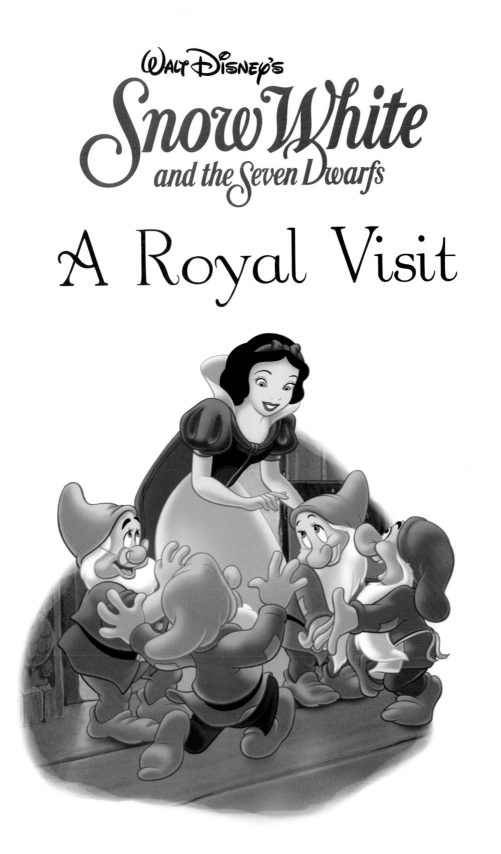

Snow White was just about as happy as a princess could be. She had married her true love—the Prince—and lived in a beautiful castle. Her wicked stepmother was gone. She had everything she could ever want. But she missed her good friends from the forest, the Seven Dwarfs, very, very much.

"Why do you look so sad, my darling?" the Prince asked Snow White one morning.

"Oh, I've just been thinking about the Dwarfs," she replied. "It's been so long since I've seen them. I really miss them."

"Well, why don't we go for a visit?" the Prince suggested. "Their cottage is not so far away."

"That would be lovely!" Snow White cried. "Let's go today!"

294

While the Prince called the groomsmen to saddle their horses, Snow White wrote a note to tell the Seven Dwarfs that she was coming. Then she asked a bluebird to deliver it.

At the Dwarfs' cottage, Sleepy was just waking up when the bird landed on the windowsill.

"Say, there's a boat in his nose. Er—a note in his toes," said Doc, noticing an envelope in the bird's claws.

"Looks like a . . . a . . . a . . . *ah-choo*," Sneezy said with a sniffle.

"Indeed," Doc replied. "But who could it be from?"

Then, just as he reached for the letter, the scent of sweet perfume drifted to his nose.

"Why, it's from Snow White!" Doc exclaimed. He and Sneezy and Sleepy ran downstairs to tell the others.

Doc began to read the note. "'My dear Dwarfs,'" he said. "Heh-heh, she calls us 'dear'!"

"Oh, get on with it!" grumbled Grumpy.

Doc scanned the note. "Well, um . . . well, golly gee! She's comin' for a visit! Today!" he cried.

"Hooray!" Happy cheered. "Snow White is coming!"

But the other six Dwarfs looked around their messy cottage. Dirty dishes and clothes were piled everywhere.

Doc handed a broom to Dopey. "We have a lot to do, men! Sleepy, you bake—er, *make* the beds. Bashful, you fold the clothes. Sneezy, you dust the furniture. Dopey will sweep the doors—er, *floors.*"

"She's comin' at *noon*!" Grumpy huffed. "She'll want lunch. Someone's gonna have to cook!"

"Why don't you and Happy fix somethin' suitable for Snow White to eat?" Doc suggested.

The Dwarfs started to work on their chores right away. It didn't go very well.

Sleepy got tired and lay down in the middle of Grumpy's bed. Sneezy kept sneezing as he dusted. And Dopey knocked furniture over as he swept.

Meanwhile, Happy and Grumpy couldn't agree on what kind of sandwiches to make.

"Snow White likes peanut butter and jelly, I know," Happy declared.

"She likes ham and cheese," Grumpy grumbled. "Everyone knows that."

By the time Doc finally got them to agree on something,
the clock struck twelve and there was a soft rap on the door.

"They're . . . ahh . . . ahh . . . *heeere!*" Sneezy sneezed.
"Wake up, Sleepy!"

The Dwarfs ran to the door and opened it. Their beloved princess was here! They smiled as Snow White hugged each of them and kissed their foreheads. "How I've missed you all!" she cried.

"Please forgive the mess, Princess," Bashful whispered to her. "We didn't quite get it cleaned up."

"Oh, please," Snow White said with a laugh, "forgive *me* for giving you such short notice! Besides, I've come to see *you*—not your cottage."

"Would you care for a ham-and-jelly sandwich?" Doc offered, holding up a platter. "Or peanut butter and cheese?"

"Oh, how sweet," Snow White kindly replied. "But . . . well . . . you see . . ." She paused. "If I had known you'd go to all this trouble, I wouldn't have brought a picnic with me."

"Picnic?!" the Dwarfs exclaimed.

"Well, yes. I remembered how much you liked it when I cooked, so I brought some of your favorites."

Just then, the Prince walked in with an overflowing basket.

"What did you bring?" Doc asked hopefully.

"Oh, just some roast chicken and deviled eggs," Snow White said. "Cinnamon bread and butter. Corn and tomatoes from the

royal garden. Sugar cookies, cinnamon cookies, and a fresh apple pie. . . . But let's eat your sandwiches first."

The Dwarfs looked at one another, and Doc cleared his throat. "We can have ham and jelly anytime," he said. "Let's enjoy your picnic and have a great visit."

And that's exactly what they did.

The End